I0819598

CHAYLEE McCLEESE

Evernight Teen ®

www.evernightteen.com

ISBN: 978-0-3695-1369-4

Cover Artist: Jay Aheer

Editor: Melissa Hosack



This is a work of fiction. All names, characters, and places are fictitious. Any resemblance to actual events, locales, organizations, or persons, living or dead, is entirely coincidental.

**CHAYLEE McCLEESE**

# DEDICATION

In loving memory of Jason Dennler & for anyone who has been stuck in a cycle of grief and found their savior through music.

**CHAYLEE McCLEESE**

# PITIFUL PEACHES

Chaylee McCleese

## Part One

*Harold Hayes: Why don't we start from the beginning?*

*Penny: I don't even know where that would be.*

*Harold Hayes: Well, when I write for Zipper, I start my piece when a band or song changes. When did everything change?*

*Penny: I suppose everything changed when I went back to Moose Creek for the Summer of 1975.*

*Harold Hayes: And?*

CHAYLEE McCLEESE

## Chapter One
### Arrival At Moose Creek

*Song: Georgia Peaches—Lynyrd Skynyrd*
*June 14th, 1975*

The sunbeams shone on my face as I sat in my mom and stepdad's old ruby pickup truck. We were packed together, like sardines in the front, but I didn't mind because I was close to my parents in ways most teens were not. I waved my hand out the window as Captain & Tennille's "Love Will Keep Us Together" played.

My stepdad, James, took his eyes off the road and said, "Penny, change the radio. This crap is awful." James was a tall man with brown hair that he brushed back. He had green eyes, a mustache I liked to make fun of, with a heavy gut. He insisted that mustaches were groovy, and he looked like a famous rockstar. Even though his appearance was far from Hollywood material, he was a star to me.

I laughed and replied, "Understood. How is this?"

The station switched from pop to 105.1 The ROCK! It played the new summer hit "Rock and Roll All Nite" by KISS. My stepdad grinned and turned the dial to thirty-two as he sang along.

I could feel the song's vibration through my feet up to my chest. I smiled back at him because nothing could change my mood. I loved all types of music, so the song didn't matter. We were also heading to Moose Creek, my favorite place in the world.

My mom, April, must have noticed my enthusiasm, because she laid her head on my shoulder and whispered, "You ready, Penelope?"

I leaned into her and said, “You know I am, Momma.”

Momma was beautiful. She had puffy blonde hair with bangs that framed her face just right.

I was taking notes about the song in my beaten-up notebook so I could write a critique about it later when my momma nudged me and said, “You better not sit around and read all summer long. Words won’t do you justice. You need to live and learn.”

It was true, but sometimes I didn’t want to go through bumpy patches to learn a lesson. Books and writing allowed me to live other lives without taking on any risks.

“I won’t, Momma. I am going to be with my friends,” I assured her. I stopped writing and closed the front cover of my notebook, slipping it and my blue pen, underneath the seat for safekeeping. My dog, Fawn, was in the back of the pickup, sticking out her tongue with delight. I put my hand on the warmed glass and told her, “It won’t be long before we arrive.”

Every summer, we would stay at my grandmother’s cabin in Moose Creek. It was my second abode. I loved everything about it. We were less than an hour away, and I got more excited with every turn. I knew that road better than any other. I took a deep breath. The air was crisper there. Moose Creek was my family’s breath of fresh air from our average lives.

We stopped at the closest rest stop to let Fawn out to go potty. As she trotted around the grassy area to take a squat, my parents and I took turns entering the restroom. I hurried through the convenience store to the unclean toilet. It was important to keep the stop times to a limit so we would arrive as fast as possible. I thoroughly washed my hands in the sink and spent too much time with the soap, so I didn’t dry my hands with the towel.

Instead, I shook my fingers out, causing water droplets to fly all over the store. I pushed the glass door open with my elbows, making the bell above the frame chime. I ran back to the parking lot, not looking back. One more hour felt like a lifetime. Fawn was panting, Momma was hungry, and my stepdad wouldn't stop talking about his urge to fish. We jumped back into the front and buckled our seatbelts.

"I can't believe we are almost there. I wish we visited more."

"Me too, but I have to work. You are lucky. Most kids don't go anywhere different in the summer. We could always send you away to some church camp instead," James, said.

"I know. Thanks for taking me. Moose Creek is a special place."

My stepdad sighed. "I guess. It is just a town, though."

"It's not just a town for her though, Honey," Momma said, running her fingers through my hair.

The poles in the back of the truck wiggled as we paved our way to paradise. Every summer, the last hour of the trip felt like the longest for two reasons. The first was that anticipation consumed me the closer we got to town. The second was that there was no radio station that could reach where we were. The radio waves of 105.1 THE ROCK! did not travel far enough past the rest stop, making there little to no reception. On various corners, a song's chorus would break through the speakers and then turn back into static. Music made things more digestible. A good song could make time pass as fast as lightning strikes. Songs had a power over me. A sad song could make me withdraw myself, while a pop song could make me giggle like a little girl. And rock made me feel all kinds of emotions at once. Without the radio, I was left to wait, with nothing to cushion my eagerness.

When the truck eventually pulled up to the log cabin, my stepdad turned the key so it would stop idling. My grandma was sitting in her rocker on the front porch, waiting for us.

Grandma was old and typically kept to herself, except if there was any drama, she became the center of it. I noticed she looked skinnier than usual. She had short gray hair, fake teeth, and a sunken face while depicting a welcoming manner.

"Could you get out so I can talk to Grandma?" I asked my mom, as I scooted closer to her so she would have to open the door.

My momma got out of the truck, and Grandma embraced me. She looked proud when she exclaimed, "My God, Penny, you have grown. Your curly blonde hair is now wavy because it's so long, and your legs are already tan!"

I peered down at my legs. Somehow, they were already darker than my usual pale white shade. Summer started only a few weeks ago, and I went swimming as much as possible.

"How have you been?"

"Oh, you know, the usual. I've been here and there," my grandma replied.

"When did you get here?"

"A couple of days ago. I had the neighbor boy help me get my bags in. It's nice to be back here. It gets too crazy in Butterfield during the summer months. Life slows down here instead of speeding up." When we ran out of topics to discuss, she held my gaze for a minute. "Go help your mom with those bags."

I liked helping out, so I ran toward the truck and grabbed a bag from the top of the tailgate. Fawn jumped out of the back and followed close behind my heels. She always made sure to be by my side to protect me.

When I walked into the familiar house, I knew my grandmother's cabin was falling apart at the seams. I could roll a ball from the kitchen, and it would roll out the front door. The floor was uneven, the walls had cracks, and the plumbing barely worked. None of us mentioned how bad it was to Grandma because she would break down and say everything was perfect. She refused to get maintenance done and liked to "jimmy rig" things. Jimmy rigging was her way of fixing things, which mostly consisted of using duct tape. In a year's time, things had gotten progressively worse. But it wasn't the house or the duct-taped pipes that made me want to come to town every summer. It was my friends, the creek, and the peaches.

Moose Creek was known for its delicious peaches. The town's population was one hundred and thirty-three people, and everyone knew each other. There was one store in the town center called the Peach Pot that sold everything from toilet paper to homemade peach ice cream. Despite the small population, many traveled to pick peaches, fish, swim, and be tourists.

Technically, no one in my family lived there all year round, except we were not vacationers either. Moose Creek felt like my home. Townspeople welcomed me with open arms each summer like I was their own, and I had met many friends over the years. I was fourteen going on fifteen, and I felt like I could finally break out of my sister's shadow.

My sister used to come with us until she moved to a big city and stopped having time for us. I craved to be cool like her, even when she acted like I was a burden. For once, it was just me. My sister wasn't there to make me feel like I wasn't enough anymore. I would go swimming, hang out at the library, go to the park, see my friends, eat peaches, and have a great birthday. Nothing was stopping me from making memories over the summer.

I laid my orange travel bag on the bed in the room I typically stayed in. The majority of the room was full of junk, or what my grandma considered treasure. My grandma became a hoarder after my grandpa passed away. She filled the hole he left with material items. After a failed attempt at owning a ceramic business, she bought things she didn't need because she claimed someday, she might need the stuff. I was shocked to find the bed was spotless and a pathway led to the bathroom. She must have worked hard to "clean," meaning she had moved the stuff to a different location before we arrived. I rubbed my hand over the moose quilt laid on the top of the bed and thought, *wow, that's fitting.*

Even though I enjoyed my time in the bedroom the previous summers, I didn't want to waste any more time reading in a congested room full of random items my grandma purchased. I only had so many more years of being a kid and wanted to spend them wisely, like my momma wanted me to. I was itching to walk down to the park and see if any of my friends were there, but I knew I had to visit with my grandma for a little longer. She was the one who let us stay, and it was the noble thing to do.

I exited the bedroom to join my mom, grandma, and stepdad in the cabin's small living room. Fawn was lying on the rug underneath my mom's feet. I bent over and gave her a mini pat on the head. She looked up at me with her bright brown eyes and wagged her tail back and forth. The furniture in the cabin was all different colors, making it look like rainbow vomit. One chair was red, the couch blue, the tables had a plain wood stain, and piles of books were stacked behind the chairs to hold them up.

"Sit down, Sweetie. Your grandma was talking

about the story of when she first bought the house," my mom said.

I shrugged but immediately fixed my obvious disinterest with a polite smile and nod.

James gave me an all-knowing look. He knew that she told the story every year. Heck, she practically said it every week. We all nodded and laughed at the optimal moments so my grandma would be pleased.

"It really is amazing that the only reason you got this house was because you gave the previous owner one of the family's recipes."

"Well, that isn't even half of it. Did I ever tell you about the time…"

In the middle of her sentence, James interrupted her by saying, "Sorry to cut in, Ma. I need Penny to get me something from the store. Would you excuse her?"

My grandma paused and said, "Oh my, sorry, I talked on and on. You know how it is getting old. Of course, go!"

My stepdad reached into his billfold and handed me a crinkled-up five-dollar bill. The bill's surface was rough and had a rip on its left side. As my stepdad sat there, I wanted to thank him a million times over. He got me out of the house without a fuss, making him shine brighter than anyone else in my eyes. I felt bad that he was stuck there with her, but I refused to stay another minute.

I grinned at him and mouthed the words, "Thank you," before I walked out of the front door with the crumpled bill in my hand. The porch made a screeching noise as I stepped onto the old, decaying stairs, and my heart beat faster, anticipating the sight of my friends and the idea of a spectacular summer.

## Chapter Two
## Fawn gets a Home

*Song: Cracker Jack—Dolly Parton*
*June 25th, 1967*

***Harold Hayes: I'm curious. How did Darren become a part of all this? How did you two meet?***

***Penny: Well…***

For my sixth birthday, there was only one thing I wanted. Down the street from my grandma's cabin in Moose Creek was a little white house with a wire fence around it. Every day, when I walked to the park with my sister, we would walk past the enclosure. Tiny puppies would jump against the fence, whining, seeking a connection.

That time, a boy was swinging on the porch swing. His legs swung forward and back as he propelled his weight. I learned how to pump myself on the swing earlier that year and admired his ability to pump so well. He was holding one of the puppies in his skinny arms.

I nudged my sister. "Who is that?"

She responded, "Penny, you need to get out more. That's Darren. He's the preacher's son. His family moved here a couple of weeks ago. I think he's about your age."

Darren looked sweet. He had short, dark black hair and a cheesy grin. He was wearing a striped, blue shirt with black basketball shorts. I wasn't too big of a fan of dressing in baggy clothes, but he pulled it off well.

My sister, exhausted from me tagging along with her, yelled, "Hey, Darren! Would you do me a solid and play with my stupid little sister? She's now a six-year-old."

Darren did a quick look over at me and yelled,

"Come play with the puppies!"

I hesitantly opened the gate and looked behind my shoulder to see that my sister had already left me. *Figures*, I thought as I approached Darren, who nodded for me to sit beside him.

His forehead scrunched up in concern. "Is your sister ditching you on your birthday?"

I sighed and sat down. It wasn't uncommon for my sister to ditch me for her friends or boys she was interested in. She refused to let me into her personal life the older she got. I was getting tired of it. I didn't understand what was so wrong with me that she avoided me at all costs.

The puppies leapt into my lap. One puppy with a black spot on the top of its head kept falling over, and the other pups would trample over it.

I turned toward him. "What is wrong with that one?"

Darren scooped up the pup in one hand. "This is the litter's runt. She is the smallest and won't fight the other dogs for food or attention. They are a border collie mix of some sort. We did not realize that our dog, Sassy, got pregnant before we moved here, hence these little guys. Sadly, Sassy didn't make it through giving birth, though. At least that is what my dad said." Darren wiped a tear away from his face.

Growing up without a parent sounded awful. I worried about the dog's well-being. I also didn't like seeing the boy so upset.

I leaned forward to pet the tiny dog when Darren set it in my lap. The pup looked up at me with her vast, glossy eyes, and I fell in love. The dog slowly licked and tickled my hand with her soft, pink, wiggly tongue.

"No one wants the runt. You can take her for free if you want. My dad wants the puppies gone as soon as possible. Maybe you could bring her around here so I could visit her too," Darren explained.

What kind of person could give up such an adorable creature so easily? I stared at him in disbelief.

"You know, I don't see why people don't like the runt. There is nothing wrong with being quiet and keeping to yourself," he said.

I clenched the pup close to my chest. "What should I name this little gal, then?" I knew I could take the puppy because my momma and stepdad had talked about getting a dog for a long time, and once they saw her face, they wouldn't be able to resist taking her in. I also related to the poor dog; she was the smallest and was easy to forget.

He laughed. "That's up to you."

I set the pup down, and her legs wobbled from side to side. "I don't know. She looks like a deer who was just born and has no idea how to walk," I said, giggling.

Darren looked at her. "I guess we have to call you Fawn then."

His tennis shoes skipped into his compact house. He came out with a yellow collar and a rope. He connected the collar around her petite neck and tied the rope to the collar. He tugged on it to ensure it was secure and handed me the other end of the makeshift leash. "Happy Birthday. Take care of Fawn for me, and swing by any time." Darren beamed.

My face lit up with a smirk. "You know I will."

****

When I walked the puppy back to the cabin, she pulled the leash too tightly, got too close to my heels, and fell over. I ended up carrying her down the street in my arms. She wasn't used to walking on a leash and would need to be thoroughly trained. I put the tiny pup under my shirt when I entered the living room. Her warm fur brushed against my stomach. My grandma, stepdad, and mother were lounging on the couch.

Their eyes darted to me when I said, “Hey. Breanna ditched me, so I came back. You know how we were talking about getting a dog sometime?”

“Seriously, she left you again? I’m sorry. What about a dog?” James asked.

“Well…” I stalled.

“Get to the point, Penny.”

I figured my words would not be enough, so I pulled the tiny pup out from under my shirt. Her little tail wagged when she saw my family. She pawed at her face, causing all of them to say, “Awe!” in unison.

“I’m sorry about your sister. I don’t know what to do with that girl. But where did you get this dog? It doesn’t have any flees, does it?” Momma asked.

“I got it from the new preacher’s house. The boy there said it was the runt, and they had to get rid of it. Can we keep her?”

“Oh, I don’t know, Sweetie,” my momma said, touching Fawn’s fur.

“Please!” I begged.

“Those are the Lawrences, right? The ladies and I investigated them, and they seemed like a fine family—religious, proper, and good neighbors. I’ve heard they keep a clean house, so I wouldn’t be worried about fleas or pests. They mostly have girls, but their boys are quite handsome,” Grandma Hartley said.

“It is her birthday,” James said, shooting his eyebrows at Momma.

“Oh, all right,” Momma agreed.

I jumped up and down and rushed to the bedroom to try and teach my new puppy all there was to know. As we grew up together, I taught her to sit, roll over, walk on a leash, walk off a leash, heel, spin, and do whatever else

I could get her to do for a treat. She made it so I wasn't alone anymore. Fawn was mine and only mine. I was responsible for her, and she took care of me. She was more than a friend. She was my connection to the rest of the world. And most importantly, she led me to Darren.

**CHAYLEE McCLEESE**

## Chapter Three
## Old Friends with New Voices

*Song: With A Little Help From My Friends—The Beatles*
*June 14th, 1975*

Rocks flew in every direction as I strolled down the gravel road. My flip-flops made a clacking noise with each step I took. Whenever pebbles stuck between my foot and the sole, I would stop and shake them out. The sky was bright blue, and white fluffy clouds hung in the distance. It had been a year since I saw any of my friends. My stomach leapt as I got closer. I didn't feel like a lot had changed. The only things that were different about me were that I grew four inches taller, my hair got longer, and I dressed myself with more style.

I saw the old play structure and the pavilion we liked to sit under. I scanned the park with my eyes for someone, and that's when I saw him. Darren was standing on the basketball court shooting hoops. He wore a black band t-shirt and holey light flare blue jeans. His hair was slightly longer, causing strands to stick up in opposite ways. He was engrossed in dribbling the ball while humming some song. I was too far away to make out the title. Darren was my best male friend. We didn't care about how one another looked, yet it was impossible not to notice how his shoulders were broader and that he was over a foot taller.

I approached him from behind by tapping his shoulder with my pointer finger.

He snapped around and looked at me up and down like I was a stranger.

Breaking the silence, I said, "Did you miss me or what?"

Darren picked me up and jumped, laughing, "Of

course I did, Copper Penny. I didn't recognize you." His voice became deeper since the last time I saw him. He went from being a falsetto to a baritone, gruff and smooth at the same time.

I tried acting like I did not notice his new voice, so I browsed the court. I ran up to a bright orange portable 8-track player lying by the base of the basketball hoop. "Darren, is that the new portable 8-track player? I can't believe you got this. We can listen to music all summer long!" I exclaimed. Portable 8-tracks were the newest way to listen to music on the go. I was jealous of his access to recently developed technology. If I wanted something new, I would have to wait months until it went on clearance, or when Momma would give in to my nagging.

He leaned against the basketball hoop pole. "Yeah, I saved up all my money from mowing lawns to buy it. It's pretty sweet. Isn't it?"

I nodded in agreement. The hot pavement scorched the bottom of my feet through my flip-flops. "We should go sit down," I told Darren, trying not to make direct eye contact with his slim face. When I got off the concrete, I slipped off my sandals and sprinted to the gazebo through the lush green grass, taking great pleasure in feeling the feathery blades against my toes.

Darren gathered up his stuff and met me at the picnic table.

When he sat down, I asked, "Where are Zach, Thomas, and Betsy?" Darren's head fell into his hands. I pried his fingers away from his face and asked again, "Where are they, Darren?"

His pupils dilated as he pleaded, "Please don't be upset. They all went to some camp in Walla. I tried to convince them not to, but their parents forced them to go. If you knew it would only be me this summer, you might not come."

I shook my head in disbelief. "You should have told me. Seriously? Summer camp?"

"Yeah, I know. I hate disappointing you. I promise to make this summer fun. We will jam out, go swimming, and I will even go to the library with you. I really am sorry."

I hit him on the shoulder. "Okay, we will make it work. I guess you're not too awful to be around."

He laughed, and we sat there until the sun started to go down. We chatted about the past year and how our first year of high school went; it was embarrassing and productive at the same time. Darren spent most of his freshman year in band while his friends got to play sports. It was interesting to see how Darren had grown up in just the span of nine months. I wondered if I changed that much, too. I hoped he didn't think I was too different.

The sky turned from blue to bright yellows and pinks. Sunsets in Moose Creek remind me of multicolored dahlias. I loved growing flowers and planted them at my house in Butterfield under our kitchen window every spring with my momma. Gardening was a passion project I rarely discussed around my friends because it was one of my spring activities. There were many parts of my life that my friends in Moose Creek didn't know about since they only saw me from June to early August. Like a tree, I was a separate person during the other seasons.

"I should get back to the cabin before my grandma rolls over and croaks. Plus, I should take Fawn out to go potty," I teased Darren.

He giggled. "Look, I know she looks old, but she is not *that* old. You really should take Fawn out, though."

I gripped my flip-flops between my toes and held up the five-dollar bill I took out of my pocket. "James got me out of her stories by giving me this to get him something at the store. I better run and grab a candy bar before they close so I don't come back empty-handed and our lie is revealed."

We went around the corner to the Peach Pot. The Peach Pot was a narrow log cabin turned into a store. The store contained five short aisles, one wholly dedicated to Peach-themed gifts.

Tammy stood behind the register, doodling on a notepad. Tammy and her husband, Paul, ran the store for the past fifteen years. They were dedicated workers aside from when business was slow. When there were little to no customers, they became burnt out and bitter. She glanced up at us as the doorbell dinged. "Welcome to the Peach Pot. Please let me know if there is any way I can assist you," she said in a robotic tone.

Darren hung around me as I looked at the new peach merchandise.

Tammy experimented with selling jackets, peach candy, sweets, and other small miscellaneous items. Whatever sold more, she would continue to make. The glass case in the aisle contained more delicate things like jewelry and keychains. There were beautiful peach charm bracelets and earrings in various metals. I liked the way they looked, but I wasn't carrying enough money to buy anything extra. My grandma would have questioned James if I brought back a pair of earrings anyway.

I approached the counter. "Tammy, it is me. We got into town a couple of hours ago. Can I get a peach chocolate bar?"

She realized who she was talking to, blinking herself out of a trance. "Oh, sorry, Penny. How have you been? The town has been dead for weeks now. Do you want just the candy bar? We got some new peach taffy, and I will throw it in a bag for another fifty cents," she said, turning around to grab the bar off the shelf behind her.

Darren muttered under his breath, "Don't. It tastes like bubblegum. I don't know what they were thinking."

I thought about it briefly. "I will pass on the taffy. Thanks for the offer, though." I never liked the taste of bubblegum. It was too sticky and potent for my liking, and I trusted Darren's opinion.

Tammy told me my total was twenty-five cents, so I handed her the five-dollar bill James gave me. She counted back my change, and I threw it all in the back pocket of my jean shorts because I didn't want to deal with organizing it. Motioning for Darren to follow me out the door, I grabbed the bar off the counter and said, "I should walk back to the cabin for the night. You better have something spectacular planned for tomorrow. You owe me for not telling me everyone went to camp. You know I would have come either way. Moose Creek means a lot to me. I will see you later."

"I don't know why you are saying goodbye. We have to walk in the same direction. Your grandma's cabin is on the same street as mine."

"I know, but I did not expect you to walk with me. I thought you might stay out longer."

Darren started walking toward our houses. He put his hands in his back pockets as he wandered. "Copper, do you think my dad would let me stay out late alone? Being the oldest of seven does not come with any fun benefits other than being a free babysitter."

"I'm sorry. At least you aren't left alone all the time. I love my parents, but they are too consumed with their stuff and think I should be too. James works and my mom, I don't even know what she does anymore."

His pace slowed as we approached his house. "That's true. My parents don't have a life. Their kids are their life. It's like instead of practicing the drums, I have to help with dinner, do the laundry, or make sure my sisters don't scratch each other to death like in cat fights. They expect me to be a parent."

I chuckled. "They are fighting for attention and love. Every girl wants to feel special."

"There's only one girl I know is special, and I am looking at her."

I knew he had to be joking because he liked to poke fun at me. "Yeah, and you are the boy of my dreams. Go to sleep, Darren. I will see you tomorrow."

The glow of my grandma's cabin windows brightened the path. I snuck back up the front porch, attempting to avoid the spot that makes it creak. I opened the door slightly.

My grandma fell asleep on the couch watching reruns of M.A.S.H., and my mom and James were already in bed.

I let Fawn out and entered the bedroom to remove my pajamas from my cramped suitcase. I slipped into my loose plaid pants and pulled the shirt I had packed over my head. Crawling into the moose quilt, I got snug and imagined what the summer would be like with just Darren and me.

## Chapter Four
## Cold Water, Warm Touch

*Song: I Feel the Earth Move—Carole King*
*June 15th, 1975*

A waft of freshly cooked sausage filled my nostrils. I yawned, rising from the comfort of the bed.

My mom was hovering over the stove, cooking biscuits and gravy.

I patted her on her shoulder. "Thank God, I am starving."

My stepdad and momma were discussing what they planned to do for the day. They were fighting because James wanted to go fishing, and my mom wanted to pick peaches.

I pulled out a chair at the rickety kitchen table and said, "Stop arguing. You have the rest of the summer to do both."

James winked at me. "Exactly why we should go fishing today!"

I rolled my eyes at him. "Where's Grandma? Isn't she typically up by now painting her ceramics?"

My mom sat down at the table with me. "Sweetie, your grandma is packing some stuff because she has to leave."

I fixed my posture by sitting up. "What do you mean? Why would she leave? She stays here every summer."

My mom laid her coffee cup down on the table. "Grandma's sister, Barb, has broken her leg from tripping over your grandma's stuff. Apparently, she was trying to bring Grandma some pie and wandered around her house back in Butterfield."

It was about time my grandmother's addiction to

collecting finally caused a problem, but why did it have to happen at the beginning of the summer vacation?

My mom got up and put a plate of biscuits with a fork in front of me.

I said, “Thanks,” and started eating. “So why is Grandma leaving because Barb was a clutz?”

My momma glared at me. “Penny, don’t talk with your mouth full. Your grandma feels responsible for Barb getting hurt and is going to take care of her.”

“What does that mean? We can’t go home. We just arrived yesterday!”

“Don’t worry, Honey. Your grandma is letting us stay for the rest of the summer as long as we leave the cabin exactly as it is.”

I leaned in and murmured, “Fine by me. I will stay out all day in the sun until I burn to a crisp to avoid touching her junk.”

My grandma joined us in the living room, causing me to think more carefully about what I was going to say. I pursed my lips together.

“What are you cooking? It looks disgusting. Too bad you do not have the family recipe for biscuits and gravy. I make the best. Penelope, let’s paint before I go back to Butterfield,” Grandma Hartley said.

I don’t know why my grandma always picked on my mom. Her biscuits and gravy looked delicious.

My mom’s shoulders sank as she scrubbed at the pans in the sink, holding her tongue.

“Sorry,” I mouthed silently to my mom as I followed my grandma to gather up some acrylic paint, brushes, mason jars full of water, and some towels to help make our creative endeavors.

She guided me to her hidden closet full of chalky white ceramics made from numerous molds she had. I chose a frog sponge holder to paint, and she took out a container with a lid she wanted to design. Then we carried the supplies out onto the deck and dipped our brushes into the thick paint we poured onto an old tile that fell off the shower. Anything could be used as a paint pallet if you let it be.

"I've missed you. You have blossomed into quite a young lady. I assume you went to go see the preacher's son the other day. I hope it was worth leaving our visit for," Grandma Hartley said as she stabbed her brush into the tile, making the bristles spread out.

"I did see Darren, but I also went to the store to get James something."

"Uh-huh. I see. Well, I thought I would do something with you since, as you have heard, I will be leaving shortly. My sister always likes to make things about her. It's ridiculous I have to take care of her because she decided to intrude on my life."

"I'm sorry you must leave. Thanks for letting us stay while you are gone. I really appreciate it."

"Oh, well, you are a part of James's life," she said, painting the container a deep red.

I painted my frog with a base coat of green and went back in with a smaller brush to add flowers to its back. I liked adding little details that weren't intended to be there in the first place. We painted for a while, listening to the woodpeckers and birds chirp. Occasionally, she would speak up and tell me another story from her past I already knew.

"Flowers on a frog? Interesting design choice. We better start cleaning up. I need to get going. Could you help me put everything into the car? You can leave yours here to dry, and the next time I come, I will glaze it and give it to you. I think I will put mine in the backseat of the car and take it with me."

"No problem," I said, holding in my breath. I

loved my grandma. However, she had changed since I was a girl. The lady who sat beside me painting wasn't as loving as she used to be. She wanted people to feel obligated to her, and I did. She was the one who owned the cabin. She was the one who held the keys to my favorite place on earth, and I wasn't sure if I did things with her because I wanted to or if I felt like I had to. I know I used to enjoy our time together, painting, hearing about her past, and drinking tea, but I wasn't the little girl mesmerized by her stories anymore. And she wasn't a kind old lady who wanted a granddaughter. Sometimes, I thought that she expected everyone else to suffer because she was hurting. She was an anchor who sunk everyone and everything she came in contact with.

I helped my grandma get her bags loaded into her green Ford Escort, kissed her on the cheek, and sent her on her way. I barely escaped without her saying, "I'm getting too old for this." I know I shouldn't have felt glad she was leaving, yet a weight was lifted off my shoulders as she pulled out of the cabin's driveway.

****

I ran back into the cabin to prepare for the day. I put on my new yellow crochet bikini top and bottoms my mom got from the discount rack. I layered my jean shorts on top of the bottoms and threw on a button-up shirt tied in the front. In the summer months, you had to be ready to go swimming no matter what. I banged my head up and down so my hair would have volume. Since my hair was naturally wavy, I did not do much to it. Then, I put on some silver hoop earrings and my silver anklet for the final touches. The anklet had little swirls down my foot, forming a toe ring. For some reason, I felt I was more powerful with that anklet.

The living room was empty. Taped to the fridge was a note left by my stepdad. The note read:

*Penny,*

*I convinced your mom to go fishing.*

*We will be back tonight. I left some hotdogs in the fridge if you get hungry. Make sure to keep rocking. Love you. –James*

I called out, "*Fawn*! Time to go! Come on!"

Fawn zoomed around the corner, wagging her tail a hundred miles per hour.

I petted her head as I said, "It's time to see Darren." I grabbed two shiny red Peppos from the fridge and went out the front door.

Fawn followed a couple of paces behind me.

When I arrived outside Darren's house, drums and cymbals were clanging, girls were screeching, a hair dryer was blowing, and static echoed from the TV. I knocked on the door twice, waiting for someone to answer. When there was no luck, I went to the basement sliding door. Through the glass, I could see Darren holding his little sister with one arm in his lap and hitting the drums with his other. He moved his leg up and down as she giggled. Darren was an amazing brother to Doreen. He spent the most time with her since she was the youngest and needed the most attention.

I waved until he saw me and unlocked the door.

He said, "Hey, sorry about that. I couldn't hear you. I was teaching Doreen how to play a song on the drums. My parents are out of town visiting another Preacher. Come on in." Doreen's hair was in two braids as she bounced around the house.

I sat on Darren's parents' pee-yellow couch. Fawn jumped on Darren and licked his leg with enough saliva to fill a pool. "Fawn, get down. So, you are home alone then? What are you going to do? Are you going to throw a rager?"

His little sister said, "Penny, what's a Rag-er?"

I laughed so hard I snorted while Darren said, "Nothing you need to know about Dory." I handed him the Peppo. He opened the can with a loud pop. "Thanks. I needed some sugar to keep me energetic," he said, slurping down the cold can of soda. Darren loved any form of sugar and caffeine. He couldn't survive without his daily dosage of sweets.

I was nervous because how could we do anything fun with all his siblings? He must have known I was getting angsty because he said, "I know I promised you the perfect day, but I have to babysit, so I have a win-win solution. We are going to swim at the creek!"

Doreen jumped up and down and screamed, "*Swimming! Beach Day! Oh yeah!*" Going to the creek wasn't exactly like going to a beach. To Doreen, a beach day was swimming in a rocky tunnel filled with water. It had all the elements a beach does, except the hot, sticky sand.

"It's a good thing I came prepared. I'm already wearing my swimsuit. How will we get there?"

He scratched his head. "You can ride on the pegs of my bike like you used to."

Doreen skipped up the stairs, hollering at everyone to put on their bathing suits.

Darren had to help the littles get ready, so I went to the kitchen to prepare lunches for them to bring. Most people would feel weird taking over their friend's kitchen, yet I didn't. Darren's parents trusted me, since I grew up eating dinner at their house every Sunday night. Darren's parents were decent people, but they could only give so much attention with seven children. Their love was spread thin, like trying to get peanut butter from the sides of an empty jar. Darren's parents criticized him more than his siblings because he was the oldest. Any way I could take the pressure off of him, I did.

I packed eight sandwiches, some grapes, and a box of ding dongs in an old tote bag I found. Darren was able to round up all his siblings at the door. I smiled at him. "Does this mean we are ready to go?"

He nodded and then paused. "Wait! One more thing." He ran into his bedroom and came back with his portable 8-track.

"Perfect."

The kids went to the side yard and got on their bikes. I made sure Fawn was okay before I went outside. One of Darren's brother, Benjamin, set her up with a bowl of water and food. Benji was only ten and liked to play Dungeons and Dragons with his friends. Gabriel, Darren's father, thought it was satanic, so Benji secretly played at other people's houses. The Lawrences were forced to sneak around if they wanted to do anything they liked that wasn't related to the church. I thanked him for taking care of Fawn and placed the tote of food in one of the girls' bike baskets. Then, I hopped on Darren's silver metal pegs. He turned his head over his shoulder, and said, "You better grab onto me, or you will fall off and scrape yourself up."

I gripped the top of his shoulders like I did as a kid, feeling his meaty arms. His shoulders were warm, and his biceps pushed out of his old shirt. When we flew down the hill at Moose Drive, the breeze blew my hair in every direction, making me unbalanced. I grasped his shoulders tighter as he shouted, "Hold on, Copper!"

After a couple of minutes, we reached the creek. I laid our lunches and towels on the bank's side. Darren's siblings were jumping off their bikes and racing toward the water. He propped his bike against a powerline pole and took off his shirt in one swift motion. He looked at me as if to say, "What are you waiting for?"

I shimmied off my jean shorts and turned away

from him when I unbuttoned my shirt and threw it on the ground. I sat on the side of the grassy bank, dipping my big toe into the water. I shivered.

"Is it too cold for you?" he asked.

I smirked and said, "Never." Pushing myself off the bank, I submerged my body in the piercing water. I couldn't help but prove to Darren I wasn't afraid.

Darren ran and jumped into the creek with force, causing water to fly into the air. His body made a hole in the creek's reflective surface.

He rose out of the water, shaking. "Geez. It is cold." As water droplets ran down his face, he brushed them away with his palm. He began to splash me. I held my breath and dove under the murky water to avoid his hits. The rocks were smooth on the soles of my bare feet. I pushed myself to the bottom and grabbed a handful of pebbles, keeping my eyes closed. I then laid my towel down on the uneven bank to inspect the nuggets. Some of the rocks I identified as mica. Mica looks like a rock with chunks of tinfoil in it. Sometimes, mica could look like a beautiful silver ring; other times, it looked like trashy leftovers wrapped in the fridge.

"Turn on the 8-track!" Darren yelled. I dried my hands on the fibered towel, then placed his Jesse Young and the Matches tape in the machine and turned it up as loud as possible. Jesse Young and the Matches was Darren, my stepdad, and I's favorite band. Darren and I sang along with the chorus. *"You need to see that I am right in front of you. It's always been me. We are like fire when we ignite, baby together, we are bright."*

Darren played with his siblings as I tanned, found pretty rocks, and listened to the album. A van full of out-of-towners pulled up next to me. The sun glared into my eyes. I blocked the sunbeams with my hand to see who they were. I could make out a teenage girl, her mother, and her younger brother. The girl advanced toward me.

I sat up slightly, causing my muscles to contract.

The girl asked, "Hey, do you guys mind if we join you?"

Darren was too busy splashing his siblings to notice them.

"I don't see why not."

The girl introduced herself and placed her fancy beach towel beside me. She had on bright red lipstick and a navy-blue one-piece swimsuit. Her hair was brown, long, and straight. She was very pretty and knew how to present herself. I asked her where she was from, and of course, she was in Moose Creek on a weekend getaway. We talked back and forth for a while. I did not care much for talking to strangers. I had my friends, and they were enough for me.

The city girl was looking at Darren a lot, making my face grow uneasily warm.

Eventually, she leaned into me and smacked her lips, gaining the courage to ask, "Are you with that boy? He is super hot! If you aren't, I am going to hit on him. There's nothing like a vacation to hook up with boys you will never see again."

I was dumbfounded. I was not with Darren. Darren was my best friend, but he was special. He deserved someone great, not some random girl. "No, I am not with him, but he's the preacher's son, so he won't mess around with anyone."

Her jaw dropped. "Yeah, not worth it. Good luck." She picked up her towel and got up. Her family was hanging out by the back of their van. She approached them and whispered, "The water looks gross. I think it has fish pee in it or some sort of chemicals. I don't think it's safe to swim in." She wanted to leave, and her family accepted her weak excuse. She gave me a fake wave goodbye as they hauled back into their van.

Darren got out of the water, dripping. He shook his soaking hair on me like a wet dog attempting to dry off. I hit him with one of the towels, and he laughed. "Okay, okay! Sorry!" he said, sitting next to me. "What did that family want?"

"They asked me for directions," I said, not wanting to talk about what actually occurred.

We nibbled on the sandwiches and snacks I packed with his siblings. Then, we played grape basketball by throwing grapes into each other's mouths. Whoever won had to pay for the next time we got ice cream at the Peach Pot. I made six baskets, which was an accomplishment for my poor athletic abilities, but Darren still won the game with eight baskets.

"You owe me an ice cream cone, Copper."

"Yeah, it's a good thing I still have the money from James. I know you won, so I will pay for your ice cream. But can you go to the library with me tomorrow, like you promised?"

"Why do you even like that place? It's old and smells funny."

"I like it because you can read and play board games, and I want to check out a book for the summer."

He turned on his side. "Fine. It's a deal. I heard they have some sheet music and comic books."

"How is drumming? Did you get any better? The last time I heard you play, it sounded like a thunderstorm with no rhythm."

"Wow, thanks for that. I have gotten better. I will have to play for you sometime. It takes a lot of work to find time to practice. My dad still sees it as a waste of time since he wants me to become a preacher like him."

"Little does he know you would much rather be a music teacher. Is that still your dream, or did high school change you? Do you know James wants to work in music production? He would be good at it. He is a great listener. Although he's always working so he's probably too busy at the lumber mill to make it really work."

"Yeah, it's still my dream. You want to be a music journalist, so we are not much different. I think everyone dreams of becoming something bigger." As rock stars and artists became more significant than life, everyone around me yearned for money, fame, and love. To feel was to live; to be average was to be as good as dead. Being a music journalist to me wasn't just a dream, it was a lifestyle.

I hoped my skin would tan well while we swam around and drowned out the rest of the world with music. I couldn't stop thinking about that girl. My mind struggled to understand why I felt embarrassed when she wanted to hit on Darren. By the end of the day, I was drained. The skin on my thighs was reddening, and I didn't want a painful sunburn during the first week of being in Moose Creek. Darren helped me pack our stuff onto the bike and let me head home without an interrogation. I got Fawn from his house, walked home, and boiled a hot dog to fill my stomach rather than getting lost in my thoughts.

## Chapter Five
## Books and Hooks

*Song: The Book I Read—Talking Heads*
*June 16th, 1975*

The library was limited but full of knowledge and wonder. Darren did not like the library because it was quiet, and he was used to the chaos of his house. I stalked the shelves, looking for my next captivating read. I was spending my days well and deserved to dive into a book. I wasn't going to lock myself in to read. I would have time to sit back and enjoy a new story when Darren was at church or was busy.

He was supposed to meet me at the door of the library. When I arrived, he was nowhere to be seen. I waited for a while, until I gave in and went inside. I was standing in the teen section, and I spotted the spine of a book titled *Are You There God? It's Me, Margaret.* The title took me by surprise. As I pulled the book off the shelf, a finger reached out and grabbed my wrist. I pulled away, snapping my arm back. When I heard Darren's memorable laugh, I sighed out of relief.

He stalked around the corner, revealing himself. "You have to admit that scaring you is hilarious."

"Hilariously mean."

He gestured toward the book I held. "What book is that?"

"It's called *Are you There God? It's Me, Margaret.* It seems interesting. I like how it's a question. I feel like that all the time. Where have you been?"

"Hey, my father's the preacher, and I still don't know what to believe. It doesn't make sense how God always lets horrible stuff happen. Music is my only God. At least it answers when I call. Sorry I'm late. My dad wanted me to do some chores before I left," Darren said with a frail shrug.

"It's all right. Music is a God I worship, too. Let's find you some sheet music." Music made me feel like I belonged. It gave my life a purpose, just like religion does for others. We went shelf by shelf until we found the music section. Moose Creek's limited library had three wooden shelves of sheet music. I picked one out from the second shelf and handed it to Darren. "This one seems like something you would play."

Darren skimmed through the folder. The song's name was "Pitiful Peaches." He held onto the file and said, "I will try it, but only because you chose it for me."

"We better check out then!"

"Uh, Penny, I don't have a library card."

I pretended to hit him with the book. "You live here. I only visit in the summer. If anyone should have a library card, it's you." Besides getting your driver's license, a library card was the most essential rite of passage to me.

He flinched. "I only go to the library when I am with *you*."

"Fine. I will use my card to check out the song," I said, disappointed in Darren's choices.

I proceeded toward the desk and asked the librarian if I could check out the book and sheet music. Her glasses were perched on the edge of her nose. Librarians liked to wear their glasses like they were looking into a microscope. Despite making it more challenging to see, it was a part of the aesthetic. If I had to guess I would say it was a requirement for the job to have bad eyesight. They probably strained their eyes from reading so much.

She looked over the top of her glasses and said, "Of course! Summer reading is important for a young girl like you."

She wrote the date and my name in the checkout log and returned the book and file to me.

"Thank you! I will be back." The only time I didn't return a library book was when Fawn was a puppy and chewed up a picture book I borrowed. I was too embarrassed to admit my fault for leaving the book on my bed, so I avoided the situation altogether by switching libraries for several months.

I found Darren sitting in a nook of the library. He was air drumming something on a shelf next to him.

I peeked around the shelf and said, "Woah! Are silent concerts the new thing?"

He stuck his tongue out at me. "Shut up. You owe me ice cream." Darren popped up and pulled my arm out the door. We walked around the corner to the Peach Pot.

When we got close, I handed Darren the money from my pocket. "You are the man. Get it for us. I want a double-scoop peach ice cream waffle cone. Get whatever you want. I will save us an outside table." Darren didn't treat me differently because I was a girl. I knew he liked doing things for people, so I let him do small unmeaningful things for me.

"All right, you need anything else, Princess Peach?"

I laughed. "No, that will be all. Thank you. Tell Tammy hi for me."

I planted myself at my favorite table. It was round, had a lovely tablecloth with peaches printed on it, and two white-painted metal chairs. A ledge over the building protected us from the direct sun or if it happened to rain. I tapped my fingers impatiently on the metal wires on the table for Darren to bring me the ice cream. Without our other friends, it looked like we were on a date.

Vacationers walked on the deck around the store. One family was stationed at the built-in fake jail cell. It was a wooden wall with a window protected by bars and a carved sign above it labeled it, "Jail." The spot captivated out of towners to stop and take ridiculous photos. A little girl and her brother were boosted up to the opening as their father took a picture of them pretending to be captive. The kids made silly faces at their mother who was observing them. I missed that sort of connection to my parents. When I was younger, I wanted to do everything with my momma and James. They were my idols. I smiled at the family as they got off the deck and walked into the store.

Darren pushed the door open with his shoulder while he carried two gigantic peach ice cream cones. He let the family go past him. I waved him over. He handed me my cone with his free hand and licked his cone in his other as he sat down.

"Sitting at a table for two makes it look like we're on a date," he said.

Dang it, he thought the same thing. "I guess it could, but who cares what people think."

"It's not a bad thing for people to think."

We couldn't be on a date; we had been friends for so long that I never thought about him in that way. I changed the subject as fast as possible. "Are your parents back in town? The Peach Play Games are next week, and I wanted to know if you wanted to be on a team with my family and me. We have been missing one person since my grandma left."

The Peach Play Games were a bunch of competitive games that Moose Creek held each June to celebrate and raise funds for the community. He continued licking his ice cream cone. "My family is back and has more than enough people. I'm sure they won't mind if I join your team for one year."

"Really? Thanks! It might be the year my family could finally win, especially if you join us."

He flexed his arms. "I am the best at peach baskets." He was great at basketball. He planned to try out for the high school team next school year since last year his dad didn't let him.

I shook my head. "Yeah. You suck at the bowling competition."

"We all have our strengths and weaknesses."

I kept licking the cold, mushy cream with the edge of my tongue. The family I saw earlier walked out of the Peach Pot with kids' cones. The children's eyes became huge, as they stared at their ice cream with hunger. I grinned as they walked hand in hand with their father. It reminded me of the first few summers I went there with James.

Darren laughed as I tried to keep up with my melting cone. "You have ice cream all over your face. You look like a little kid."

With a mouth full, I said, "I know."

He leaned over the table and used his thumb to clean my face. I felt a chill throughout my body, but it wasn't from a brain freeze.

## Chapter Six
## James

*Song: I Can Help—Billy Swan*
*August 5th, 1964*

***Harold Hayes: And how about James?***
***Penny: Do I have to write about him?***
***Harold Hayes: Yes, you should write it. Art is pain.***

When I was three years old, my father left. My momma, my sister, and I were barely making it by. We were struggling because my mom did not work. The most she ever did was sell Avon on the side. We stayed with one of her friends, hoping that something would change so we could eat something other than noodles with butter every night.

Then, she met James. James possessed a hardness to him that made him seem more mature. My mom knew of him because they went to the same high school their junior years. One day, they ran into each other in the grocery store. My momma came up short at the register, so she started putting back a can of beans when James handed her a dollar bill. "Don't worry about it. It's on me," he told Momma, saving her from disgusted looks and a plain dinner.

The first time I was introduced to James, we visited the city park. In the center, a band played, trying to use their musical talents to make money. I played on the playground until I got curious enough to sit with Momma and him. My sister stayed on the playground, minding her own business. Kids screamed joyfully as they slid down slides, swung on the swings, and played hopscotch.

James grabbed my hand and walked me over to the band.

My mom waited on the bench, twirling her hair around her finger. She got a tube of lipstick out of her purse, applied it to her lips, and pressed her lips together, ending the whole scene with a pop of her mouth.

James started dancing. He spun me around and tapped his feet to the strumming of the guitar. The band cheered us on as we whirled around in circles. I chuckled as each note juddered my earlobes.

"I know your name is Penelope. I think I will call you Penny, though. Why don't you throw a penny in this band's hat and make a wish?"

"But it is not a wishing well!" I yelled.

"You are wrong. This hat holds all of these men's dreams, and it can also hold yours." He pushed me toward the hat, and I threw the penny in, wishing my mom could be happy again and her new relationship would work out.

James threw in a couple of bills as well.

"What did you wish for, James?" I asked him with my curious sponge of a brain.

"I wished that I could be someone to you and your mom. I wished I could be a great father like my father was to me."

After that, things did change. James rented us a baby blue-painted house twenty miles outside of the city. He worked at the lumber mill and provided for us. My mom learned how to cut hair and did it on the side. Every chance we got, James and I would listen to music together. Things in the kitchen also changed. We could buy anything from the grocery store. My momma made roasts, chicken, soup, salads, and more. We were far from being rich, yet we felt like we had won the lottery.

I knew James wanted a family, to protect, love,

and cherish. Except he couldn't have any children of his own because he was sterile. At times, I speculated if my sister and I were enough. In July 1968, James and I were listening to music in the living room while my mom was out of the house shopping. We were scooting around on the hardwood floors in our socks. All of a sudden, he moved the needle off the spinning record. The room fell silent, and my body went slack.

"Penny, I need to ask you something," he stated with his hands on his hips.

"Okay, but after, can we turn the music back on?"

"Certainly. I wondered how you would feel if I asked your mother to marry me. If she says yes, I would be your stepdad."

"If you will be my stepdad, then you can marry my mom," I said as I placed the needle back on the track, scooting my feet along the cracks in the wood.

My momma and James got married in the fall. It was an intimate wedding. I got to be the flower girl. I walked down the aisle and threw marigolds I picked from our freshly made garden. That day was the first day I felt I could finally let my guard down. James and my momma were scared that he would be drafted, but I didn't worry because James was there to stay. I knew my wish would come true. Every time The Selective Service System conducted a lottery, my mom would sit around the television set anticipating his birthday to be called, but it never was.

James was kind and helped anyone who needed it, except for helping himself. Occasionally, he got into what my mom called "funks." And no, I do not mean the type of music that makes you groove. When James was in a funk, he did not talk to me and spent more time at work.

Things got worse when James's father passed away. I was ten years old, and death seemed miles away.

At the time, I did not understand the permanence of death and how it could leak into your life until it consumed you.

On his worst days, James would hide in his bedroom and tell Momma, "Go away. I need to be left alone." If she didn't let him be, he would get angrier and yell, "I said *go away*!"

She would sheepishly surrender into our spare bedroom, and he would sink into his pillow, spending his days in a haze. I didn't blame James for his sadness, nor did I blame my grandma's reaction to her husband's death. Everyone was hurting in their own way, and I lived on, like kids do.

As I got older, I became more independent. My momma wanted me to do things by myself. Teenagers should spend more time with their friends than their parents, so I did what I could to be normal. I focused on having sleepovers, spending time on my hobbies, making friends, and doing well in school. The time I spent with James got shorter; when we came together, it was for music or celebrations. So that's why I couldn't wait for the Peach Play Games. The competition made it so we would finally be back together for a shared goal.

## Chapter Seven
## The Peach Play Games

*Song: Stand By Me—John Lennon*
*June 22nd, 1975*

I spent every day with Darren. We went swimming again, hung out at the park, and prepared for the Peach Play Games. I was halfway through reading my library book, and Darren was working on learning how to play "Pitiful Peaches" on the drums. I asked him multiple times if I could hear it, but he would only let me once he perfected it. The days were getting longer and hotter. Although I was having a great time with Darren, I missed my other friends. I needed to talk to Betsy more than anything. She would know why it bugged me that a girl hit on Darren. I convinced myself it was because I wanted to protect him, not for another reason.

To enter the Peach Play Games, you needed a team of four players. Each player from a team would sign up for a game. Darren signed up for peach baskets. I signed up for bowling. My mom was going to bake peach crumble bars for the sweet treat competition. James signed up for the sawing contest. We were prepared. The team with the most winners received free ice cream from the Peach Pot for the rest of the summer and a brand-new pedal boat!

On the day of the games, I sprung out of bed with a spring in my step. I was more than ready.

Darren came over early in the morning to get his team shirt.

"Good morning, Darren, the basketball star! Are you ready to win a pedal boat?"

"Of course I am. We will use that boat the rest of the summer," Darren said, matching my enthusiasm.

James handed Darren his sage green shirt. The shirt was soft and contained black letters embroidered on the back stating, “Hartleys.” My grandma made the shirts before she left.

“If we win, I am going to use that boat to go fishing all the time. Don’t worry though, you guys can come with me when we win,” James gloated.

Darren shook his hand. “Hey, this is your family, James. You can use the boat however you like.”

My stepdad smiled, but it did not reach his eyes.

My momma was preparing water bottles to keep us hydrated throughout the day. The competition started at ten o’clock, so it was almost time to leave. She gathered the drinks and her peach crumble bars and entered the front of the truck.

Since there was not enough room for all four of us to sit, I sat in the bed of the pickup truck with Darren. When the truck turned, gravity made Darren’s leg slightly graze mine. A jolt of electricity flowed through my body. I pulled my leg closer to my chest and swung my arm out the side as the wind brushed my bare face.

Team check-in was in front of the library. My stepdad signed us in and paid our dues, before we headed to the basketball court for the first game. Darren was practicing shooting air hoops as he waited in line. One by one, each contestant would get a bucket of peaches to throw in the basketball hoop. The contestants had to stand in a line twenty feet away from the hoop and throw as many peaches as they could in one minute. Whoever made the most peaches in the basket would win the round.

Darren’s brother, Benji, went first. He scored two peaches in one minute. We cheered him on to show our good sportsmanship. I was proud of him for doing his best. After three more people, it was Darren’s turn.

Darren approached the line and bent his knees toward the lined pavement. The judge started the timer and blew his whistle.

"Ready, set, go!"

Darren grabbed two peaches at a time and threw them at once. The first two swooshed into the basket with speed.

The crowd gasped.

"Are you allowed to do that?" one observer asked.

"No rules have been broken. Darren can continue," claimed the judge.

Darren bent his knees again, grabbing two at a time. I stared at him in amazement. He made eye contact with me as he threw them, and they fell to the concrete. The crowd became still. He wiped his hands on his shorts and tried again. He focused on the basket, and the peaches flew through the air. They hit the rim at the last second and bounced forward into the hoop. The timer beeped, and his turn was over. He'd made four peaches into the basket. Two more people tried to beat his record and fell short. Darren was announced as the winner of the 1975 Peach Baskets Game. He ran up and hugged me with a slight squeeze.

I was a fresh peach in his hands, but I was not ready to be picked.

"One game down, three more to go, Copper," he said with a grin.

I pulled away from him. "Momma is next."

The sweet treat competition took place under a gazebo in the park. We huddled around the picnic table as the judges tasted each recipe. My grandma typically made her famous peach cobbler for the contest. My mom improvised since she was not there, and Grandma refused to give her a Hartley recipe because she wasn't blood. My mom's peach bars tasted similar to Grandma's creations, so I was assured of my mother's dish even when she wasn't.

The judge started at the beginning of the table, tasting each treat with consideration. Embellished pots and pans lay decoratively on the table, making each treat look delicious. When he got to my mom's bars, he paused. His eyes watered, and his nose flinched. He got to the last treat on the table and scribbled on his notepad. They told the spectators that the winner would be announced in five minutes. The judge conversed with his family and city council to have them taste each sweet treat. After what felt like forever, the judge said, "The winner of the 1975 Peach Sweet Treat competition goes to April Hartley!"

"Oh, my! Thank you. I did not expect this." My mom rejoiced as the judge elevated her arm to represent her victory. Winning a baking contest wasn't just a small triumph for my momma. It was important. Grandma Hartley was the one who could bake and had all of the secret recipes up her sleeve. She didn't think my mom was a good enough baker for her son, but this gave Momma the confidence she lacked. Her smile widened as people complimented her dish.

The bowling tournament was next. The palms of my hands were sweaty. I couldn't stop thinking about Darren. We lay in the grass and shot gunned a ton of water until we felt hydrated under the beating sun. I began to not feel so well. Every time I looked at Darren my heartbeat quickened. I didn't know what to do. Why did he have to look so good? Before I could think, my family was encouraging me to get in line for the Peach Bowl.

"You got this, Copper!" Darren said.

I waited stiffly on the hard ground for my attempt. The Peach Bowl had the same rules as bowling, except there were only five rounds instead of ten. The lane was constructed out of a smooth tarp and glass soda bottles. The judge ensured there were no rocks to disrupt the flow of the peaches.

I stepped forward, got into position, moved my arms back, and let go at the right time. Four out of ten pins fell to the ground. In my peripheral vision, I could see Darren jumping up and down.

"Yes!"

Four pins were great for a single roll. Peaches do not weigh much, so knocking down glass bottles with the sweet fruit was challenging. However, when I made eye contact with Darren, I lost all concentration I came to the competition with. My legs were weak, and I couldn't breathe. It was like he was undressing me with his eyes. I bowled my second try and missed all the remaining pins. I sulked to the back of the line.

Darren waved at me and mouthed, "You got this. Shake it off." I couldn't shake it off. I did not know what I was doing. How could I be sure of myself if I was in denial about liking my best friend? Each turn got worse and worse. Darren and my family kept shaking their heads in frustration. I was ruining their chance of winning the pedal boat. I detested letting them down, but how could I focus when all I wanted was to squeeze Darren's shoulders again or kiss his soft looking lips?

I was not surprised when, at the end of the final round, they announced that one of Darren's sisters had won. I was dazed and confused.

"Penny, I think you have heat stroke. You do not look too great. Darren, sweetie, could you take her somewhere to cool off? Make sure she drinks lots of fluids," my mom said with a concerned look.

"No, Momma, I will stay to watch James compete. Then I will go. I promise."

My mom grudgingly nodded as she led James to the Peach Tree Saw contest. The sawing contest was the simplest one. Whoever cut through a peach tree trunk the fastest won. It was an easy task for James, so I wasn't worried. Darren and I watched from a distance as the whistle shrieked.

James moved the saw back and forth as if his life depended on it. Sweat dripped down his forehead, and his motion slowed. The ridges on the saw stopped cutting through the wood. His cheeks sparkled, and for a moment, the sweat resembled tears.

Darren's dad, Gabriel, was catching up to him.

"How is my dad—" Gabriel's log broke into two pieces with a loud clunk!

"Darren, I think your dad just won," I said, astonished. Gabriel had scrawny arms that fit into suits for preaching, not cutting logs. The Hartleys and the Lawrences tied for the 1975 Peach Play Games. The judge and our parents formed an intimate circle. We watched in uncertainty as they talked in hushed tones.

"Okay, we have reached an agreement! The Hartleys will take the new pedal boat, and the Lawrences will receive free ice cream for the rest of the summer! What an amazing compromise, folks! Thank you to everyone for coming out. Supporting this town helps us grow," the judge said.

Darren and I gazed at each other. We held back until the crowd became less dense. "Let's get you back to the cabin, Copper. You need to rest. I have never seen you mess up bowling so bad. Ice cream is on me the rest of the summer."

He pretended to help me walk to the truck like I was severely injured. He acted like nothing had changed between us, but I was an awkward mess.

My momma and stepdad were seated in the front

and were unaware we were at the back of the tailgate.

"I am tired of this. I wanted to win those stupid games for my family, but I failed. I failed at my day job! I need to do something else," we overheard James say.

"It was just a silly competition, and we won the boat you wanted. Isn't that enough?" my mom asked.

"Do you know why I slowed down? I slowed down because I thought of my dad and how he was the glue of my family. Without my dad, my mom has gone crazy. We just ignore her hoarding problem. She guilts me every time we stay here. She reminds me I will never live up to him, and staying in that room drives me insane," he sputtered.

"I am sorry. I did not know this was on your mind. We can't leave yet. Penny would be upset. We can head home sometime after her birthday."

Darren knew I could not take listening to their private conversation anymore. He loudly hit the tailgate and jumped in the back. "Hey! Everyone did great today! Why don't we take Penny back to the cabin? I think we all could use some rest."

"I agree, Darren. Thank you for joining our team. You are a peach," my mom said, concurring with him as the truck rumbled up the gravel path.

****

When I got home, the phone rang. I took it off the wall and answered. "Hartley's residence. Penelope speaking. Who am I talking to?"

"Penny! First off, I am so sorry I went to camp. My parents forced me to go, and although I miss you like crazy, you won't believe what has happened," Betsy screeched.

"Hey, Betsy! It's okay. I miss you too. How's camp?"

"Camp has been … interesting. I sort of am now

dating Thomas," Betsy said.

"What? How did that happen?" I asked.

"I don't know. It's like one day, he looked different to me. I realized that he is kind and funny, and he listens. One thing led to another, and we are going steady."

"Wow. I don't know what to say. I am happy for you two."

"So, how's Moose Creek with Darren?" she pried.

"A girl hit on him when we went to the creek, and I felt weird. Plus, I might have to go home sooner than expected. It's all screwed up. This summer was supposed to be perfect," I admitted.

"Why do you have to leave? You aren't making any sense. Explain more."

"Fine." I explained everything. I described every second I spent with Darren so far. From the first night I arrived, down to our knees touching in the pick-up.

She listened without judgment and then she spoke. "You were jealous. You like him. It's that simple. You have to tell him before you leave."

"No. That can't be it. Tell me it's not," I whined, hoping she would tell me the opposite.

"It is. I got to go. I only have so many phone minutes to use. You need to get out of your mind and see where life takes you. You can't avoid something because you are afraid. Darren is a good match for you, and he adores you. You should tell him how you feel, then maybe you could end up like me and Thomas. Have a great birthday! Night."

Betsy lived life on the edge, while I liked to live grounded. I had dreams like everyone else and wanted to make connections, but loving someone was different. Loving someone meant opening a world of hurt I didn't want to face.

The phone made a busy signal and went to the tone as I slammed the phone back onto the hook. I took a deep breath. My world was falling apart. I liked Darren, and my stepdad was miserable. I wasn't ready to leave yet. I needed to figure out what I wanted and fast.

## Chapter Eight
## Birthday Bonds

*Song: Sister Golden Hair—America*
*June 25th, 1975*

It was my 15th birthday. Birthdays are odd because it's the day people are supposed to treat you like you are unique. It's also a day when you are supposed to make these unreasonable expectations. Still, you end up being disappointed with someone or something. I refused to be disappointed by others on my birthday. Nothing could top the day I got Fawn. I owed it to Betsy to take her advice and seize the day, because I wasn't sure when I would have to leave Moose Creek and return to Butterfield.

I got out of bed, brushed my teeth, and removed my hair from the curlers I put in the previous night. I thought about the girl at the creek, and how much effort she put into her looks. I wanted to look that good for Darren. When I saw myself in the mirror I felt like Farrah Fawcett. My hair had a bounce to it. I went through my bag and pulled out my green floral dress. The dress lay just above my knees, had a fitted waist with a brown belt, and flared shoulders. I applied lipstick to my bottom lip, rubbed my lips together in a circular motion, patted down my skirt, and entered the kitchen.

"Oh, my! You look so grown up. Happy birthday, my sweet girl," my momma said with a huge smile.

"It's nothing, Momma. I am the same old Penelope."

"That's not true. You are simply glowing! James! Get in here and take a picture of our beautiful fifteen-year-old!"

My stepdad entered the kitchen and stuttered,

"You are *really* pretty. I am proud of you. You look like your mom."

"Thanks, James," I said, hugging him.

His strong arms grasped around me like a teddy bear.

My mom ran into her bedroom and came back with a small gift box. The box had a funky chevron print and a shiny bow on top. She urged me to sit down and open it.

I slowly undid the bow and removed the lid off the box.

Inside the box was a fragile locket in the shape of a peach. The locket contained a picture of my mom, Fawn, and James inside. The only place you could buy something so sentimental was in the peach gift section of the Peach Pot. James and my momma must have had the necklace custom-made. I had seen similar jewelry in their glass case, but nothing like what lay in the tiny box before me.

"You guys, this is the best gift I could have asked for. Thank you so much," I said, pulling the chain up to put it around my neck. I wanted to wear it everywhere. It was stunning. "Could you help me close the latch?" I asked James.

The metal was cold against my bare chest when he draped the necklace around me. I lifted my hair out of the way as my mom clasped her hands together, gazing at me.

"What are you waiting for? Take her picture, for heaven's sake. I have to remember this," my mom commanded. .

James backed away from me and picked up our Polaroid camera. "Cheese!" he said.

I smiled with my teeth as the flash blinded me. I was squinting in the photo. My eyes were strained and pinched together.

“Darren wants you to go over to his house as soon as you get up. He said he had some sort of surprise for you. You better go,” my momma told me.

“What does he have planned?”

“That is top-secret information,” she said, rushing me out the door as fast as she could so she wouldn’t tear up.

****

Darren opened his front door immediately as if he had been waiting by the door all morning. He wore tan cargo shorts and his most excellent crimson button-up shirt. Most of Darren’s clothes were worn until they couldn’t be worn anymore. His parents got his clothes secondhand, or Darren’s father would give him the clothing he grew out of. The crimson shirt he wore was in great condition. He must have bought it himself.

“Hey, birthday girl.”

“Hey. What’s up? My mom said I needed to be here when I woke up.”

Darren guided me inside his house. He led me into the basement and told me to sit on the couch because he wanted to show me something. He grabbed his two drumsticks and sat down on his stool. Even though I loved music, there was something awkward about having someone play or sing for you. It was more intimate than seeing someone naked because they had to strip away all of their creative layers. I rarely let other people read my writing because it was personal.

“Please don’t make fun of me,” he begged as he lifted the sticks. He started hitting the toms at a steady beat. Darren sang as he played.

*“Pitiful Peaches are what I am to you.*
*We can swim at the beaches.*
*But my love is still true.*

*Pitiful Peaches keep me alive.*
*I would bleed for you.*
*Baby, we must survive.*
*Pitiful Peaches are sweet but tart.*
*Baby, baby, baby,*
*Please don't squeeze my heart.*
*Pitiful Peaches are what I am to you."*

The song continued into a solo drum sequence. It sounded like rock n' roll combined with a loving pop song.

I stared at him in awe. "Is that the sheet music from the library? That sounded great! You've got a knack for playing the drums."

"Uh, thanks, Copper. I thought since it was your birthday, I would finally play it for you," he said shyly, setting down his sticks and taking a breath.

"I don't recall the sheet music having any lyrics or solos. Did you write those lyrics?" My heart palpitated. Did he like me too? It was ridiculous. This was Darren. The Darren I had known forever. I needed to get my act together and play it cool.

Darren would not look me in the eyes. He mumbled something under his breath.

I decided not to pry too much and asked him if he had any other plans for the day. Betsy told me to tell him how I felt, but I wasn't ready to open that can of worms just yet.

"It's your birthday. What do you think?" he said with excitement. "How's that book you are reading about Margaret and God?"

"I finished it last night. It was a silly novel about puberty. I think it was really about identity. She struggled to fit in because she didn't have a religion to guide her."

"You don't need to worry about that. You know who you are, but remember, you are a nice Christian girl at my dad's house," Darren reminded me with a foolish wink.

"I know. It's just sometimes I wish I had something to follow and give me hope other than music."

"My dad believes in God completely and still struggles. I don't think religion fixes everything."

The thing about religion was that it gave a person loose guidelines about basic morals, but a book or a church could not tell someone who to be. Only you can choose that. Daren was trying to choose his own path, but his dad suffocated him with his own beliefs.

We did our typical birthday traditions, including getting peach milkshakes, playing basketball in the park, and playing board games with his siblings.

Dusk was approaching, and Darren said, "We need to go to the creek soon. Your surprise awaits."

When we reached the creek, I was shocked to see James was unloading his ruby-red truck. The brand-new pedal boat we won from the Peach Play Games was in the back.

"Thanks for the help, James," Darren said.

"Anything for my birthday girl. I will leave you two to it. See you in exactly an hour," James said, closing the tailgate and driving off.

Darren convinced me to get into the boat first. They unloaded the boat at a shallow part of the creek where the water went up to my calves. I carefully placed myself into the boat and put my feet into the holes to pedal.

Darren held the boat steady when he got in. He pedaled with his feet so we would propel into the broader part of the creek, which was more like a lake. Then he dropped a heavy rock with a rope tied around it into the middle of the water. Things were changing. It was just the two of us.

"What is that for?" I asked, raising my eyebrows.

"This is the best place to watch the sunset. We needed an anchor."

It was perfect. The sky started turning into cotton candy. Darren's quiet presence made me secure. I occasionally glanced at him to see if he was looking at me, too. Each time we made eye contact, we would look away from each other. I didn't want to say anything stupid, but I gained enough courage to ask him the question that kept popping up in my mind.

"Why did you do all of this for me?" I asked.

"At this point, I think it is obvious. I am sorry I could not bring your birthday present here. I will give you it tonight when I walk you home. I got you a portable 8-track of your own since I saw you eyeing mine," he explained.

He liked me and I liked him. It wasn't a figment of my imagination. It was real.

"Darren. I'm scared of doing something that will mess up our relationship," I said.

He leaned in, grabbed the back of my neck, and gently stroked my hair. A gust of pine trees and peach lip balm overcame me. I had known Darren since I was six and never got as close as I was to him. I could see every pore in his face, his three speckles of moles, and the crease of his smile. My body shivered when his lips touched mine and we kissed.

"You can't mess it up if I mess it up first," he said, pulling away.

"What do we do now?" I asked, picking at my cuticles.

"Let's figure that out some other time. Look at the stars."

We stargazed for over an hour. I was happy I didn't have to figure it out. I couldn't lose one of my closest friends over a stupid teenage romance.

Darren cut off the rope and peddled us to the shore so I could get home and warm up, but James was nowhere to be seen.

"I'm sorry. He probably lost track of time," I said.

"That's okay. It happens."

By the time James got there, my legs were completely frozen. He didn't explain why he was late or apologize, so I helped put the bikes and the boat in the back and didn't talk to him. I doubt he would've heard me, even if I spoke. The ride back was silent. Then he dropped us off at Darren's house, and I went to the door while they unloaded the bikes.

James finally broke the silence and asked us, "Did you guys have fun tonight?"

"Yeah, I think we did," Darren said.

"That's good. Take care of her like you always have. See you in a bit, Penny," James said before speeding out of their driveway toward my grandma's cabin, leaving Darren and me alone again.

Darren met me inside on his sun porch. He handed me a bag with the portable 8-track inside—this 8-track was avocado green instead of orange. I couldn't wait to use it. Although I loved my record player, it was bulky and stationary. I could use it anywhere: at the pool, while I worked in my garden, at my friend's house, anywhere. I hugged him slightly too long, and he escorted me back to my cabin. The cabin lights glared and masked my view of the front porch.

I couldn't believe I was falling for Darren.

"You better go in. I hope you had a good birthday," he said.

"The best," I assured him.

He started staggering to his house, and I couldn't help turning around and dashing toward him. He stopped in the darkness, unsure of what I would do. We stood there for a few seconds before I kissed him on his cheek.

"Thanks," Darren said, blushing.

I jogged back toward the steps. For the second time in my life, my birthday exceeded my expectations because of Darren, but I was really worried about James.

## Chapter Nine
## Fishing

*Song: Fish Song—Nitty Gritty Dirt Band*
*July 16th, 1967*

***Harold Hayes: You might as well introduce your friends as well at this point.***

***Penny: Fine. I can do that.***

On July 16th, 1967, the same summer I got Fawn and turned six, James and I went fishing. We headed out early in the morning with our tackle boxes, foldable chairs, lunches, bait, and poles. I wore James's work hat to block the sun from my eyes. The sky ended up overcast, which can cause the worst sunburn because it gets you when you least expect it. Everything looked gray from the low-hanging clouds lurching over us.

My mom made me lather on layers of sunscreen before leaving the cabin. I convinced Momma to tag along. She refused to come unless she could wear her favorite tan vest with many pockets. We looked like real fishermen, rubber boots and all.

James said he knew just the spot to get tons of bites. He took us to a secluded campground with a nice, sturdy dock hanging into the fish's habitat. We set up camp on the dock. Momma laid a blanket out for her to sit on while James and I placed our chairs at the end of the wooden plank and stuck worms on the ends of our hooks.

I was the worst at casting. Each time I cast the line, I would end up tangled in some weeds, another person's line, or my hair. James threw back his brawny arms to give me a shot at catching a fish. He then cast his own pole, and we waited.

The trick was to reel your line in just a bit as time passed. Eventually, we caught a couple of fish that were too small to keep or eat, so James let them go.

James liked to fish alone. When a handful of kids showed up, he was ready to pack everything up and call it a day.

One of the boys I recognized as Darren. He was carrying around a slimy green frog he'd found and shoving it in some girl's face as she screeched at him.

James saw my fascination with the group and said, "You should go talk to them."

I overlooked them from a distance. I wanted to make new friends, but I didn't know how to make them outside of a school setting.

"Get that thing away from me," the red-headed girl yelled.

Darren chased her around the campground as he hollered, "It's just a little froggy. He wants a kiss! It will turn into a prince!"

A boy stood up for her, his hair so blond he looked bald. "Knock it off, Darren. She doesn't like it."

I approached the group with caution. Another boy with a heavier build stood by the firepit, waiting to see how the situation would unfold.

"I like frogs," I said with a weak voice. I was not sure if my words would be enough, or if they would think I wasn't worth hanging out with.

"Oh hey. Penny, right? Guys, this is that girl I gave the runt to."

The other children looked at me.

The redhead got up in my face. "Another girl? We have to be best friends. Oh my God. I can't believe this, Darren. You didn't tell me the person you gave the pup to was a girl! You look okay. If you lose the hat, you will look better," she said, taking off my cap.

I was confused and flustered by the interaction.

"I am Betsy! I live in town. Where do you live? Do you like to paint your nails? My mom will let us paint our nails if you stay at my house..." The girl rambled on and on about the future and her likes and dislikes.

I could barely get a word in before James checked in on me.

"Do you know these kids?" James asked.

"Darren gave me Fawn, and I guess this is Betsy. I don't know the blond boy or the other one."

"Ah! I see. Well, let me talk to your mom and see if we could stay a bit longer so you could play with kids your age," James said, turning his back toward me to discuss it with my momma, who was still lying on the dock. He hollered back, "All right, we will stay another hour. I will watch your pole for you!"

I was scared to leave James and Momma. I was used to being around them all of the time, and leaving them was hard. But it was nice to have other kids to play with. I learned the blond boy was Thomas, and the other was Zach. We used sticks to dig into the dirt and make mudpies. We pretended like we were at a restaurant and that Betsy was the customer we had to please. Betsy sat on a log demanding a five-course meal as we made mud cakes, pies, and salads out of leaves and rocks for salt.

James caught a larger fish, skinned it, flayed it, and approached our group. "Do you kids want actual food? Why don't we grill up this fish Penny's pole just caught? It's a big one!"

My new-found friends cheered as James grilled up my trout. Making friends was easier than I thought.

We cut the fish into tiny pieces and distributed them among all of us. James knew I was starting to get lonely. My older sister had her own group of friends she wandered off with every night, and I was always left alone, without any place to go.

That day our group's bond formed. By the end of the evening, Betsy and I had already scheduled our first sleepover, and we all planned to go swimming together the next day. I wouldn't have to stay with my grandma and do chores for her anymore. Betsy, Thomas, Zach, and Darren weren't flawless friends, but they gave me a life outside my family, and James was the one who encouraged me from the sidelines.

# Part Two

## Chapter Ten
## Jesse Young

*Song: Fox On the Run—Sweet*
*June 26th, 1975*

After dropping off my book into the return slot at the library, I sat beside Darren on the wooden picnic table under the gazebo. I held Fawn's leash tightly around my wrist. She was lying on the turf, staring at us.

There was tension in the air, and nothing could help us because our relationship had changed, and I would probably have to leave Moose Creek in less than a week. I tried to think of all the different ways to start a conversation about what happened. My brain remained empty, and my mouth couldn't form any new words.

Fawn stirred like someone was behind us.

Before I could whip my head around, hands covered my eyes, and a squeaky girl's voice said, "Surprise!"

Betsy removed her hands, and my eyes adjusted to the light. Betsy stood before me. She was tall and had auburn pin-straight hair cut to her chin.

Following close behind her was Thomas. Thomas looked like he could be one of the Beach Boys. Most boys grow out of their blond hair after puberty, but Thomas was still blond as ever.

They sat on the opposite side of the table from us.

I was relieved by their presence. Every previous summer, they were there to even out the playing field. Instead of a duo, we were a group.

"Thomas and I decided to come home from camp

for the week to visit you! Zach stayed at camp. He told me to tell you to party on," Betsy said.

"So, how is it going steady?" I asked.

Thomas started to speak, and Betsy shook her head at him. "We have been amazing. I like being with Thomas," she said with a smirk.

We chatted about how they got together, and my stomach felt like a spinning record. According to Betsy, Thomas helped her build a birdhouse at camp, and while they glued the sides together, their hands touched, forming a deep and sensual bond. I prayed to any God that would listen that we would not talk about Darren and me. I was not ready to figure everything out, let alone gloat about it.

"I am sorry for missing your birthday, Penny. I wanted to come back yesterday. I begged for a ride from everyone I knew when my stupid parents wouldn't come and get me. I did get you a little something to make up for it, though," Betsy said, squealing. She motioned for Thomas to take the present out of his pocket.

He pulled out a sharp-edged box that resembled a deck of cards.

"Thomas told me that Darren told him he got you a portable 8-track… And I know Elvis is your guilty pleasure, so I got you an 8-track of his best hits! Sorry, I couldn't wrap it up for you," Betsy explained.

"I hope you like it. I helped Betsy pick it out on our way back from camp," Thomas said, placing the track into the palm of my hand.

I thanked Betsy properly, with our best friend handshake we made when we were younger. Whenever I stayed the night at Betsy's house, we had the routine of painting our toenails while watching Elvis' various appearances on television and gawking over his black hair, deep voice, and our attraction to him. When he was in his prime, he was a heartthrob. After a while, he struggled with health problems, and his music died out as bands like the Beatles overtook his throne. I loved the new bands and era of rock n' roll, but I admired the musicians who paved the way for them, and Elvis did that. Rosetta Tharpe and Chuck Berry inspired Elvis. Music is a cycle of inspiration and adaptation.

"Elvis? Really, Copper?" Darren asked with a smug tight lip.

"Yes. Elvis is an important man," I said, secure in my beliefs. I was happy to admit my love for Elvis if it meant I didn't have to tell the group about the kiss Darren and I shared the night before.

A shiny silver bullet rolled across the street. It was a brand-new airstream. Everyone stopped talking to look at it. It was gorgeous and had to cost a fortune. No one with that much money would be caught dead in Moose Creek. Moose Creek was a tourist town for people who could not afford a fancier getaway. The door of the airstream flew open. A man walked out smoking a cigarette. He had a brown shag-like mullet, tattoos all over his arms, a mustache, flare jeans, and a tight shirt with a deep V-neck.

My jaw dropped.

Darren grabbed my hand under the table and pinched the skin on my thumb.

The man was Jesse Young, the lead singer of Jesse Young and The Matches.

"Darren, pinch me again. This cannot be real."

"Pinch me because I think we all are having the same hallucination," he gasped.

Jesse Young paced back and forth while he inhaled his cigarette. He looked stressed.

We frantically planned to walk by him and see what he was doing. We got up and pretended to stroll by his airstream. I maintained a casual composure as my heart thrashed out of my chest. When we got closer to him, Fawn yanked on her leash, causing his eyes to land on us.

"Do you folks know of a place where I can park my airstream? I am in need of a campground," Jesse said, looking around him. "I also have no idea where we are."

We were all too scared to say anything.

Darren stepped up. "Hey, man, there are many free camping spots around the creek. I can show you if you want."

Ordinary people would not agree to go to a secluded place with a bunch of strangers, but Jesse Young was not ordinary. He dropped his cigarette on the ground and stomped it out with his boot heel. "Well, we have some room in the stream for you guys. Hop in, and my manager will follow your directions."

We did not have to talk to each other to know we would get in without hesitation. It was a once-in-a-lifetime opportunity. We would deal with the consequences later. Hanging out with a rock star was precisely the sort of memory I wanted to make.

The airstream's interior was all wood, with a bright orange breakfast booth and chairs.

A woman who looked to be in her late twenties was lying on the bed in the back, laughing at nothing.

Jesse ordered us to sit down and make ourselves at home.

Fawn sniffed everything in the new place with her wet nose. I slid into the breakfast booth with Darren. He laced his fingers into mine, and I did not jerk back. I knew I hadn't told the group what had happened yet and would have to soon. My time was running out.

Betsy goggled her eyes at me, questioning my actions. As an alternative to my normal response of panic, I accepted the unknown. If Jesse Young was here, it had to be a good sign.

Jesse yelled for his manager to come in.

A skinny man with a long gray beard and straggly hair opened the door. "What do you want, Jesse?" the peculiar man asked.

Jesse said, "Ron! Meet my new friends. They are going to guide us to a camping spot! This is uh…"

"I am Penelope, but you can call me Penny. This is my uh … friend, Darren. The redhead is Betsy, and her boyfriend is Thomas."

"Well, there you go! You can't say we are strangers now," Jesse said with a laugh. "Let's get this show on the road!"

Darren explained to Ronny how to get to one of the campsites around the creek. It was private enough for Jesse not to be spotted. "Thanks. This town is a great place for Jesse to blow off steam. As long as you guys keep your mouth closed about his whereabouts, he will be safe," Ronny said like he was attempting to convince himself more than anything.

"Do you guys all live in this tiny peach town?" Jesse asked.

"Everyone except Penny. She comes in the summer with her family," Darren said.

"This town has charm, that's for sure, but it is just a getaway. Living here would be too quiet for me," Jesse remarked.

"Sir, I'm trying to stay cool. We know who you are. I cannot lie to one of my idols," Darren admitted.

"Ah, that's too bad. Sometimes it's nice to be a nobody. At least you have good taste. If you dig music, we live for the same reason. People who live for music are different."

"I, for one, don't know much about you, Jesse. I

listen to pop more than rock. Darren and Penny love rock, though. They obsess over your songs all the time," Betsy said.

Thomas gave her a side look. He understood subtlety, even when Betsy did not.

"Darren loves the drums on your tracks. He plays pretty well when he practices," Thomas added.

"Really? Drummers can be great, but sometimes they can get on your nerves. Keith, our drummer for the Matches, was great until he got an ego. The asshole thinks he deserves more. Ron, he gets me. He told me to pack up my stuff and come here so I could think. Do you ever just need to get away to think?"

"I do all the time. I am the oldest of seven siblings, and my dad's a preacher. The chaos keeps me alive. Penny taught me how to live in the quiet, though," Darren revealed.

"I don't talk much about my personal life to the magazines or the fans. I will give you the inside scoop, since you are helping me out. My old man was a hard ass, too, so I can relate."

Betsy and Thomas started talking to each other in muffled, flirtatious voices.

Jesse motioned toward them. "New lovers?"

We nodded. "I got one, too. I picked her up before we left the city." He hollered, "Hey, Sweet thang in the back. Come on out here and meet my new friends!"

The woman stumbled down the hallway onto Jesse's lap. She had darker skin, black curly hair, and bright green eyes. "Hello, beautiful babies. It's nice to meet you. I am glad Jesse invited you to camp with us. The more the merrier," she said, kissing him passionately.

The airstream stopped with a screech.

I pulled back the curtain and saw the familiar

campsite. Darren had directed them to the spot where James and I liked to go fishing and where I had met my friends all those years ago. It had a fire pit, two picnic tables, an outside grill, and a small dock to swim or fish from.

Jesse jumped up and kicked the door open. He drank a generous amount of air and said, “This is a superb location to plant our roots! Thank you, Darry! You folks have to stay here for a while. Ron! Start a campfire.”

## Chapter Eleven
## Bonfires

*Song: One of These Nights—Eagles*
*June 26th, 1975*

Darren and I gathered sticks to put in the fire pit. We stumbled around, finding twigs and breaking off branches from fallen limbs. We arranged the twigs in a cone shape like I had seen James do, and Ronny lit them on fire with his lighter. The fire did not catch, so Jesse came blazing out of the airstream with a can of gasoline. The gasoline swished around in the red can as he flung it around.

"Be careful with that," Ronny instructed Jesse.

"Yeah, Ron, you may be my manager, but you are not my babysitter!" he hollered as he carelessly poured it. The fire burst into flames.

"That is more like it!" he howled.

Thomas and Betsy helped Ronny get some lawn chairs from the back of the truck that hauled the airstream. They spread out the chairs in a nicely formed circle. We sat down and anticipated Jesse's next move. I wanted to please Jesse in every way I could. His music changed me and James's lives.

Jesse started humming a tune. "So here is the thing … I am considering starting a solo career. The Matches don't match my energy anymore. It's like this fire here. You can have a ton of matches and sticks, but only gasoline gets it going. I am that gasoline."

"That is up to you. I don't know what The Matches are like in real life. I do know the tracks sound harmonious. The drums add a steady rhythm, the bass adds this darkness, the keyboard makes you feel like you are falling in love, and your voice brings it all together," I said, worried he would be offended and wanting to still admire his work.

"You are right there, my dear. The music is great. Life becomes difficult when friendships turn to coworkers, though. That's what I am doing here. I got to think this completely through."

Ronny adjusted his posture, making him slouch more. I thought that famous musicians would have bodyguards, not straggly managers to take care of them.

"You guys seem like friends. Have you been friends for a long time?" Jesse asked as he leaned back in his chair.

"Penny met Darren when she got her dog, Fawn. Then Darren introduced us all when we were about six or seven. We hung out every summer after that. Small towns bring people together," Betsy said with endearment.

"Ah. Nothing is like childhood friends. My bandmates Keith and Mason were some of my pals from fifth grade."

"Baby! Let's go swimming!" the woman with Jesse cut in. She slipped off her shoes, unbuttoned her jeans, and ripped them off. She rapidly threw her shirt on the dock and dove into the water.

I was amazed. She was going to swim without any thought of a bathing suit. She did not care that her undergarments would be seen. She wanted to swim, so she did. It boggled my mind how someone could be that free-spirited.

Jesse raised his hands in the air. "The woman gets what she wants!" He stripped down into his checkered boxers in the middle of the dock, revealing his hairy chest.

"Should we join? I don't have a swimsuit, but I think we would look weird just standing here," Thomas said dubiously.

Darren shrugged his shoulders. "This is Jesse Young we are talking about here. If we stand here, we might miss out on something we will never get to experience again."

I stood there frozen in time. Betsy asked if she could talk to me privately, so we walked over to the bushes. "What is going on with you and Darren? I saw you guys holding hands under the table. I am your best friend. You can't keep these things from me!" she said, shaking my shoulders.

I knew I would have to explain myself. I wished it wasn't right then, but Betsy was right. She came forward about her and Thomas. I had to fess up. "Please don't tell anyone. We kissed last night. I don't know if we are together, so please don't pester me with any more questions. We are taking it slow. I really don't want to strip in front of him. That would make things even more weird. I think we are leaving soon and don't want the last time we see each other to be hardly clothed."

"Remember what I said on the phone the other day? You have to start living now! I am super proud of you for getting some. It is about time you started showing interest in a boy other than Elvis. I promise to keep my lips sealed as long as you go swimming, so be a big girl and take off your clothes."

There was not much difference between wearing a bikini and my bra and panties, other than the fact that one was more nerve-wracking. The situation was unbelievable. I typically wore a swimsuit under my clothes every day in the summer. But I was preoccupied with talking to Darren and spaced my own rules.

Betsy was the first to strip. Thomas followed shortly after. Betsy wore a pink lace bra that stood out from miles away. When Darren removed his clothes, it gave me the courage to do it, too. I looked down at my tighty whities with disappointment. Why couldn't I be like Betsy? She knew how to impress boys and used her power without hesitation.

As I wrapped my arms around my body to hide it, Darren whispered, "You look beautiful." I blushed as he picked me up by my waist and tossed me into the water.

"You jerk," I said with a gasp. The water was more refreshing than cold. I urged Darren to join us.

He jumped right next to me. The water rippled around his body, splashing me. I lay on my back and floated, trying not to think about how I was being perceived. I wondered if my mind would ever be as light as my body when I let it become one with the creek.

"Does floating feel like crowd surfing?" I shouted to Jesse.

"Sort of. Both are peaceful," Jesse said as he floated with me.

We swam for a while, soaking up the sunrays while they lasted. Thomas and Darren had a cannonball fight that Jesse judged closely. Darren was a fierce competitor, and Thomas knew how to make huge splashes. The boys hit, wrestled, and made fun of each other while we girls pretended to do water aerobics on the other side of the dock. I spun around and tried to do front flips. Betsy showed off her famous handstand, and we all clapped like she won a Grammy. We split when the boys ruined our elegant dancing by jumping onto our side.

I floated on my back until I saw the woman sucking onto Jesse like a leech. I looked toward my friends for an escape and comfort. But I saw Betsy wrap her legs around Thomas, while snogging him. Darren noticed my misplacement and treaded water to get over to me.

"Why don't we dry off by the fire, Copper? We should check on Ronny."

He knew me too well. He knew that it was a boundary I did not want to cross, and he respected it. Most boys wouldn't care what I wanted.

Darren placed his denim jacket around me like a shawl so I could warm up.

I slipped on my clothes from earlier and sat cuddled up in his coat as the flame's heat dried my legs. I was happy we stopped swimming because the mosquitoes started flying around the grounds. The little bugs were the bane of my existence. I swatted some away with my hand, avoiding their bites.

"This is crazy! Look, I know this is not the time to talk about it, but I wanted to let you know that I am willing to be your boyfriend. We can work the distance until we are out of high school, and our friendship can stay the same. We will just kiss sometimes if that's okay…"

"Can I get back to you on that? I want to think about it. I like the kissing part, though," I said as I leaned in and kissed him. His wet lips radiated heat. It was a lot to think about. If it worked out, we would be high school sweethearts. If it didn't work out, I would lose one of my closest friends. Some part of me still saw it as weird to kiss Darren. In my head he was still that little boy who gave me Fawn.

As a teal Volkswagen bus rushed into the campsite, I drew back from Darren's lips. The headlights flashed, and the brakes squealed when it came to a halt in front of us.

Ronny stepped out of the airstream to check out the commotion, and Fawn pranced up to me.

"Who is that?" I asked.

Ronny placed his hand on his forehead, flustered. "That is the Matches."

## Chapter Twelve
## The Matches

*Song: Stuck in The Middle With You—Stealers Wheel*
*9:00 P.M.*

Ronny's eyes bugged out of his head, and his leg twitched like a runner preparing for a race. "Oh, Shit. What am I going to do? Jesse is going to flip."

The first person to get out of the bus was a man with curly light brown hair and a soft baby face. We knew this man as the keyboardist for the Matches. His eyes were content on the cover of every album.

Ronny frantically asked him, "What are you all doing here? You know Jesse needs time to cool down."

"Hey, Ronny, chill out. Keith just wants to talk to him. I came here to mediate it," the man said in a peaceful voice.

"Mason. I love you, man, but now is not the time," Ronny said, trying to persuade him.

Mason Alexander gestured with his hands, saying there was nothing he could do.

The other door of the bus flew open. A woman's leather high-heeled boot stepped onto the dirt. Tonya Stirling was the group's bass player and the only Brit in the band. She wore a short blonde pixie haircut with a teased top and had ice-blue eyes. Tonya had on an all-black, sparkly shirt with a mini skirt.

I moved uncomfortably in my seat when she pulled her sunglasses down on her nose to view us. What would they think of me?

Keith Knox, the band's drummer, scooted out of the bus seats behind her to see what she was looking at. Keith wore flared orange pants, a cropped shirt, and had an afro. He made bright colors look rebellious and stellar.

The Matches did not look like they belonged in a band together. Jesse looked like a child doodled on him, Mason wore only browns, Tonya was as mysterious as the night sky, and Keith was extravagant. They did not have a similar style or mood. Still, for some reason, they fit together like puzzle pieces that needed to be corrected yet fit anyway. They were a mistake that stuck. The band was plentiful of stardom and power. What I didn't know was that, even the brightest stars could fall to earth.

"There isn't much that can be done at this point. I am going to take a nap in the stream. Good luck," Ronny said as his voice trailed off.

Mason, Tonya, and Keith marched up to us with swagger. Fawn jumped onto Mason's legs.

"Woah! Little guy! What's your name?" he asked as he petted her fur.

"Her name is Fawn," I yelped out.

"Well, *she* is a cutie. Where's Jesse?" he said, like he was on a mission.

"Blimey, Mason, don't give the kids the third degree. Can't we just talk to them a bit?" Tonya said with her British accent. I had never met someone with a British accent, and her voice surprised me with its quick wittiness.

"It's okay. Jesse is swimming with some lady and our friends on the dock. There's a small trail leading down to the water through the clearing of trees," Darren informed them while pointing in the dusty trail's direction.

Keith plopped down into the aluminum lawn chair next to us, making the intertwined fabric strings sink. "Thanks, man. Why don't we let him swim longer? Maybe Ronny is right. How did you meet Jesse anyway?" Keith asked as he poofed up his curls.

"He asked us for directions to a campsite and took

us along," I said.

"Jesse never was the safest. He doesn't think about how strangers can be dangerous, but I guess you are just a couple of kids," Mason said.

"It's fine. These guys seem fine to me. What are your names?" Keith asked.

"I'm Darren."

"Hi, I am Penny. Our friends swimming are Thomas and Betsy."

"Nice to meet you guys. Sorry you had to meet us during Keith and Jesse's tiff. You caught us on a bad night," Tonya said with a snicker.

"What do you guys do for fun around these parts besides swimming?" Keith asked.

"Moose Creek is known for its peaches. You can go peach picking or get some peach ice cream," I suggested.

Keith checked his cream-colored watch. It had to be around nine o'clock at night. "We've got time to waste. Peach picking it is."

The Matches rose out of their seats. I did not know what to do. Darren and I should have been home. Our curfew was at ten o'clock, and I had not checked in with my family the entire day. I felt guilty. James should have been there, too. It was his favorite band. I didn't want to ruin the moment so I didn't ask if they could drop me back at the cabin. A little longer couldn't hurt. Momma and James would understand if I told them about Jesse and how I couldn't pass up spending time with a rock n' roll band. James would've done the same thing, so why couldn't I? I was sure they would know I lost track of time and was safe. If they were worried, they most likely would have called Darren or Betsy's house. I still had time before they were actually concerned.

I murmured to Darren, "I want to go but feel like

we shouldn't."

Tonya yelled, "Come on, you guys. Your friends will be fine for an hour or two!"

Fawn dashed to catch up with the group.

"It's one night. We will face the world tomorrow," Darren said as he scooched into the Matches' bus.

## Chapter Thirteen
## Nectarine Nights

*Song: Ob-La-Di, Ob-La-Da—The Beatles*
*9:45 P.M.*

Mason was in the driver's seat as Keith tried finding a radio station that was not static.

"You're not going to find anything. We are too far out," I told him.

Keith sighed and stopped fidgeting with the controls on the dash.

I was next to the window. The gigantic pine trees blurred as we flew down the dirt road; gusts of debris shot up as the tires rolled.

Fawn lay in my lap, falling into a deep slumber. Fawn used to be more energetic, but she wasn't the young pup who could run around for hours on end like she used to be.

I had no idea what would happen next. What did rockstars do when they weren't entertaining the masses or shooting covers for magazines?

Darren sat beside me. He took multiple deep breaths because he was sitting by Tonya, who, although friendly, was intimidatingly cool.

The bus had tan-colored rows of seats like short church pews. I was twirling the chain of my peach locket around my pointer finger, the image of my family tucked away yet close to me.

"So, how has Jesse been acting, Penny?" Keith asked, facing his body toward the back.

"He seemed on edge when we first met him. That girl he's with seems to keep him busy and not as stressed," I said, wondering how much I should reveal about the situation.

"You don't have to be scared. He does this every couple of months. He gets tired of sharing the fame. Let me guess. Did he tell you he wants a solo career?" Keith asked with spite.

I nodded. Was fighting a common occurrence for the band?

"Hey, man, I'm sorry. I have to admit. We are huge fans. I started learning to play the drums because of you, Keith," Darren shared.

"That's sweet. When Jesse and I were younger, we played songs for fun. Keep it that way."

Mason added, "There is nothing wrong with being okay with where you are right now."

"Those two have no idea what they are talking about. How old are you two anyway?" Tonya asked.

"Old enough," I said.

Tonya smirked at my response.

I knew I looked young. I had a babyface and chub that I couldn't shake off despite swimming all the time.

Darren looked his age though; his tall legs made him a giant for going into his sophomore year of high school.

We talked about peaches and how to tell if they were ripe. Most orchards were closed, so we had to be quiet if we were to go. It was common for teens to climb the fences to Nate's Nectarine Farm and break in for late-night shenanigans. My sister used to take all of her summer boyfriends there. She never let me tag along, so I would stay at the cabin reading until she snuck back in through the window. I still don't know if I stayed up because I was jealous or if I waited to ensure she got home safe.

I knew breaking into Nate's was wrong, but I sat in a bus with The Matches and Darren, and everything with them felt right.

The bus gradually pulled by the entrance gate to the orchard. Darren directed the band to park the bus under some shaded trees to conceal it.

I woke Fawn up from her nap and put her back on her leash. She shook herself awake as she stretched her legs and jumped out.

Tonya slid the door open, revealing the contrast between the darkness of the night, and the brightness of the moon.

"I will volunteer to climb over the fence and unlock the gate for you guys," Darren said.

"A man who takes action. I like it," Tonya joked.

Darren was like a stealthy cat and hopped over the fence with grace. He snuck around the large wooden engraved sign and opened the gate. The metal latch made a hollow wail when it rattled open. The orchard was empty. The trees sang a low song as they danced in the wind, calling out to us in an eerie yet delicate way to pick their fruit.

Mason opened the trunk and took out a guitar case. The front of the case had wild yellow buttercups painted on it.

"Why are you getting that out?" I questioned.

"We need something to collect the peaches. Don't we?" Mason asked.

I tried to hold in my laugh. "That will work. I love buttercups. Who painted them?"

"Tonya's girlfriend painted it for her," Mason disclosed. He grabbed the handle of the case and gently closed the trunk. The rest of the gang entered the orchard's wicket with caution. We sped up our strides to meet the others. Nate arranged hundreds of peach trees like young military men who got drafted. The straight rows went over my horizon line, showing an endless number of peaches.

"How does this work, anyway? I haven't been to any peach orchards in Britain," Tonya said.

"Since we do not have a ladder, we must pick the low-hanging peaches and hope for the best. Mason grabbed your guitar case to put them in. We might as well get started," I said.

Mason placed the case onto the ground and kneeled to unlatch it. He lifted the top open. The yellow paint was iridescent in the dark. "Funny to put peaches in this case. Typically, it only carries guitars and money."

Tonya grabbed a round; flush-colored peach suspended to the left of her. She pulled it off its stretchy stem and tossed it into the container. "This is bollocks! If I knew it was this easy, I would pick fruit more often. Let's fill this baby to the top!"

Everyone's fingers fixated upon hand-picking peaches one by one. Mason offered to hold onto Fawn's leash. He sat under the tree's branches with her, playing.

Fawn loved the extra attention from her new friend. She rolled on her back, demanding belly rubs and scratches.

Even though the peaches we were getting were in decent shape, I wanted to pick a ripe batch above them. I pointed up at them as I asked Darren, "Wouldn't those be so much better? I wish I could reach them."

Darren grabbed my legs, putting his head in between my thighs and boosting me onto his shoulders.

"Put me down! What are you doing?" I screamed.

"Helping you get those peaches. Now, be quiet before you wake up the entire orchard."

I steadied myself on his shoulders. His warm hands wrapped around my legs. "Give me a warning next time. You nearly made me poop myself."

Keith was watching us and laughed.

We formed a system where I would pick a peach

and drop it into Darren's hands, Darren would throw it to Keith, Keith would toss it to Tonya, and Tonya would put it in the case.

As we got into a tempo, I unconsciously began singing. "Pitiful Peaches are what I am to you. We can swim at the beaches. But my love is still true."

Darren's eyes shot up toward me.

Keith held the peach in his hand, bringing the line to a standstill. "What song are you singing?"

"Um..."

"It's a song I wrote from old sheet music I found in the library," Darren said.

"Can we hear the rest?" Tonya asked.

"Sure. Penny can sing it. She's a better singer."

"Are you sure?" I asked him.

He nodded and almost knocked me down. I caressed his hair as I gulped. I did not know how to sing particular notes or chords. I sang in the choir in elementary school. Still, other than a sprinkling of Christmas concerts, I needed more professional experience. There was no way out of singing. If I didn't sing, I would leave Darren hanging, and if I did sing, they would realize I didn't have vocal talent. My voice was juvenile and faint as I sang Darren's lyrics, "*Pitiful Peaches keep me alive. I would bleed for you. Baby, we must survive.*" By the end of the verse, my voice cracked, and embarrassment washed over me. Every member of the Matches gawked at the lyrics I sang.

"That is something else," Mason said.

"It's a catchy little snippet. I would love to add some bass to the tune. It definitely has potential," Tonya said.

Keith started dancing around and singing the lyrics at the top of his lungs. Each band member yelled the tune with him. Darren's body radiated optimism and promise. Hearing so many people connecting reminded me why I loved James so much. James introduced me to the world of rock. People with no sense of direction could feel like they belonged. Music had the power to baptize people's souls.

Mason had a hold of Fawn, making her dance with his hands. Her tiny paws swung back and forth to the Matches' voices. Tonya was lying in the dirt pretending to play a guitar as we enjoyed the moment.

I swayed with the trees, our voices, and the breeze. I closed my eyes, letting my mind soak up the full experience. I didn't want to forget a single second. When my eyelids opened, I saw two things. The first was red and blue flashing lights. The second was Fawn escaping Mason's clutches and running away.

## Chapter Fourteen
## Speed and Greed

*Song: Sweet Emotion—Aerosmith*
*10:30 PM*

The local sheriff was patrolling around the orchard. His lights flashed as I debated my next move. Moose Creek had one officer who took care of the town during the off-season. When it got super busy, like on the Fourth of July weekend, some officers from the county next to us would also patrol the area. Thankfully, it was not a busy weekend. That meant it was only Douglas.

Sheriff Douglas's favorite pastime was writing speeding tickets. The biggest threats he dealt with included attending town meetings, yelling at people for littering, dressing up as Santa during Christmas time, and onc time shooting a duck on accident. He claimed that the duck was endangering a child nearby. Everyone knew thc duck wasn't a threat, yet he got away with it because what are small town cops for?

Fawn saw the lights and bolted toward his car. Her long legs glided through the trees, making it almost impossible to keep up with her. Her yellow leash dragged behind her as she pranced. I had to think fast. I knew Fawn would come back to me eventually, but I still needed to do something about Sheriff Douglas, so I formed a plan in my head.

"Darren, you have to put me down and hide," I whispered. I crawled off his shoulders and whispered to the rest of them, "Hide! Hide! I have an idea." I did not have time to ensure the band did as I told them. I sprinted after the blur of white spots and yellow cord, screaming, "Come back, Fawn!"

Fawn was heading toward the gate we

conveniently left open. Was I the last person in? I should have closed it. I wasn't thinking enough. One single mistake like that could be detrimental.

Sheriff Douglas's car crept up to the entrance to stop. He turned off the ignition and his headlights, and the world became dim once again.

I slowed down, wheezing for air to time it exactly right.

Sheriff Douglas stepped out of his vehicle with authority. He wore a tan uniform, a brown textured cowboy hat, and black work boots. He straightened his spine as he said, "Little lady. What are you doing in Nate's Nectarine Farm at this time of night?"

"I'm sorry, Sir. My dog got off her leash as I was walking back to my campsite, and she ran into that peach orchard, so I was forced to go in and find her," I lied, finally catching Fawn in my arms.

My fingers shook. I was anxious to lie. I had to play the part of a scared girl because police are trained to tell if someone is misleading them. I was a frightened girl, just not in the way I pretended to be.

Sheriff Douglas was known in town, yet our paths had never crossed. I was lucky, he didn't know who I was.

I tucked my front curls behind my ear. "Am I in trouble, Officer? It won't happen again. I promise. Please don't tell my parents! They said I could only get a dog if I were responsible for it. Oh God, now they will take her away!"

"Calm down. It's okay. Tell me how the gate opened."

"I don't know, Sir! It was open when she ran through. Maybe the owner left it open."

"Okay. Don't worry. It will be all right. Do you need a ride back to camp?"

"No, thank you, Officer. I will take my dog straight back," I said, making sure Fawn's leash was connected to her collar and walking toward the direction of the campsites. I ambled, waiting for Douglas to leave in his car. He watched me for a while until, eventually, he closed the gate, got in his vehicle, and rolled down the road. When I knew the coast was clear, I hurried back into the orchard toward the band and Darren to enlighten them on what I had done. We had to leave swiftly before Douglas looped back around the orchard and unraveled my string of lies.

"I didn't know you could lie like that, Copper." Darren chuckled.

"It was more of a slight fib. I can lie, when necessary, but I don't like doing it. Can we please get out of here before I panic?"

"You did nothing wrong. We took fruit from the land we were born on. There is no reason to feel guilty for taking something that grows out of the ground," Keith said.

Whatever the band or Darren said could not make me feel better about the circumstances. Nate's farm would not struggle financially from missing twenty peaches, but stealing was not something I did. I was the one who suggested going there and picking the peaches, and yet I felt on edge. Teenagers did stuff like that all of the time. I needed to get my head on straight if I wanted to be with the band. Sneaking in to steal peaches was child's play compared to what The Matches were used to.

Tonya latched her guitar case and carried it back to the van.

Darren locked the gate after we went to the other side. Then, he jumped the fence.

I wondered if Darren felt guilty, too. He seemed at ease, calm, and collected, while I was scared.

When we reached the bus, I was burnt out. I missed my privacy and seclusion. My mind struggled to know what I wanted. I wanted to be with the band, I wanted to be with Darren, but something in my gut told me it was wrong. When I was with them, I felt on top of the world one minute, and the next, I wanted to hibernate in a hole.

We squashed together on the bus. Tonya grabbed each of us a peach to eat on the road.

Darren passed me one.

I smiled at him to let him know I would be all right as I accepted the peach into my hands. It would take me a minute to compose myself.

Tonya bit into the peach. "Bloody hell. This is amazing. You all need to take a bite," she said, astonished.

Dark pink juice squirted down Keith's chin as he dove his teeth into his peach. He opened the door and spit the peach out. "That's disgusting. Mine was sour." Mason laughed at him. "Whatever. Take a bite, and we will see who is laughing," Keith said, pushing the peach to his chest.

"I will. I am not weak like you," Mason said as he bit into his peach. Mason's face scrunched up as he chewed and looked like he was trying not to throw up. His adam's apple bulged when he swallowed the piece whole. "See, that wasn't so bad," he said, holding in a gag.

"Uh huh," Keith said with sarcasm.

"I guess it's our turn," I said.

Darren held up his peach and clinked it with mine. "Cheers." We both plunged into our peaches. Mine tasted sweet with a hint of tartness. The fur of the peach skin tickled my face. It was ripe, juicy, and did not gush on me. The peach was perfect. It didn't even need a pinch of sugar. I debated with myself if stealing was worth it. A peach like that was rare. I rotated my torso toward Darren to address him. "How was your peach?"

"It was okay. Tastes like an average peach."

I wanted to tell him that mine was spectacular and made me feel like life was worth living. I didn't because Mason frantically tried shoving the key in the ignition hole as his hands shook.

"Are you okay, Mason?" I asked.

"You guys might want to hold on. We have company," he said, shooting his head back.

"Great, it's Sheriff Douglas," Darren said, grinding his teeth.

Mason put his foot on the gas pedal and brought it down to the floor. The bus plowed forward at full speed. Mason yanked the wheel.

Tonya's body weight slammed into Darren, and Darren slammed into me. I was being smothered. As quickly as we fell, we were jerked to the opposite side. My body felt relieved, because Tonya was holding our weight.

Once the bus was turned around, we gained momentum. We were driving down the dirt path at eighty miles per hour. I wanted to scream. How did I get myself into a mess like that? Before then, I never lied to a cop, let alone got in a high-speed chase.

"I'm scared, too," Darren whispered in my ear.

Of course Darren was worried. He had unfeasible expectations to live up to, and his dad would be ashamed of him. If Gabriel found out he stole, he would hide Darren in the basement and make him babysit for the rest of his life. Sheriff Douglas may not have known me, but he knew Darren and Darren's family. Sometimes, I got lost in my problems and worries and forgot the people around me worried, too.

Every turn felt like Mason was beating us with a whisk to make scrambled eggs. I wasn't even sure that running away was the most successful tactic. We could have lied or hidden again.

Tonya yelled at Mason, "Would you quit giving us whiplash? Do you even have a plan?"

"Yes, I have a plan. Stolen peaches are not the worst thing a cop can find on this bus!" he screamed. I was not an idiot. I knew everyone smoked weed and did drugs, especially rockstars. Still, I liked to think that The Matches were different. Drugs were far from my mind. The only time I thought about them was when my school held say no to drug assemblies, where I was forced to see its dire consequences.

"I didn't even think about Jesse's pot," Tonya said with a sigh.

Keith shook his head. "What's the plan, Mason?"

"I am going to lose him when the road breaks into two. I am not going to endanger a couple of kids," he said, focusing all of his attention on the road.

I hated it when people just saw us as kids. I like being naive. I chose to be that way. My sister grew up too fast. Maybe if she didn't, she would have actually hung out with me. I tried to be a kid for as long as I could possibly be.

When we drove through the fork in the road, Mason acted as if he was going to go straight. At the very last second, he jerked the bus to the other road. The instruments and gear in the back clashed together as the bus's wheels rose into the air and landed back on the right path. Sheriff Douglas's car zoomed past us, its lights flashing a warning. He was chasing nothing except the night sky. It wasn't hard to outsmart Douglas.

"See, I always know what I am doing. I take care of the band," Mason said. He leaned back in the driver's seat to take a break and wiped the sweat off of his forehead crease. Finally, he placed his hand on the passenger seat's headrest, put the bus in reverse, and drove back to camp using the lesser-known roads.

Sheriff Douglas was not the most intelligent creature in Moose Creek, but it was odd that he turned away from us. Maybe he needed more energy to deal with us and fill out the paperwork for the report. Either way, I didn't want to know. I was just grateful we escaped without a scratch.

"You two, okay?" Mason prodded.

"Yeah. I'm glad we didn't get caught," Darren said, breathing heavily. His dad terrified him.

"Yeah, I don't think that cops are our real problem. Let's hope that Jesse is calm enough to talk when we return," Keith said.

## Chapter Fifteen
## War and Peace

*Song: Dancing Barefoot—Patti Smith*
*10:50 PM*

Jesse, Thomas, Betsy, and the woman from earlier sat around the dwindling campfire.

Jesse's face rose with rage when his eyes met Keith's.

Keith groaned. "Here we go."

It was strange and not like Betsy to remain quiet. Her lips stayed shut like they were taped together. Something was wrong.

Tonya slammed the door shut, and the sound grappled with the silence. The fire hissed and was careful not to crackle. Darren and I hung back to use the Matches as our shields. We did not want to be the first person to say something.

"Hey, Jesse. We brought you some peaches. We even had to run from the cops to get them for you, but you are worth it," Mason said.

"You can't butter me up with some peaches, Mason. Plus, you stole my new friends," he said, pointing to us.

My heart boomed. I gnawed on my fingernails as I peeked around the Matches' towering, skinny bodies.

"Look, I know the show didn't go as planned last week, but we are all here now and want to figure this out as a band," Mason pleaded.

"Maybe I would if he would talk for himself. Until then, I am going to be with my beautiful lady here," Jesse said as he rubbed the woman's arm.

Keith stepped forward, making the dirt compact under his boot to form a deep-lined print. "I am here. We can talk."

Jesse grabbed the glass beer bottle from under his chair and stood up. "What do you want?" He took a sip, swishing the liquid around his mouth while he swallowed.

"The show we played in Portland was rough. I am sorry I did not listen to you and follow your lead. The song order was wrong, though. The crowd would have gone wild if we had played it the way I wanted. We have to try new things if we want to keep rising in popularity."

Jesse shook his head back and spit on the ground. "My way is the right way. It's the way that works. I started this band, and I wrote that setlist. You are being ungrateful."

"I wanted to help with the setlist and write songs for the album. You wouldn't put them on it. It's not only me. We all want a say," Keith said.

Jesse looked at Tonya and Mason, gritting his teeth. "You two are a part of this, too?"

"Jesse—"

Tonya didn't get to finish before the bottle in his hand sailed through the air toward us. It was the color of moss and was translucent enough to almost shine.

Mason put his hands in front of us to push us out of the way. He was like a crossing guard guiding us to safety.

Tonya stepped back when the glass hit the ground. The dirt absorbed most of the impact, making a thud rather than a shattering noise. Multiple shards were left to poke and dig into the dirt.

"What do you think you are doing? Are you trying to hurt somebody?" Mason shrieked. His eyes glossed over with a twinkle of fear and hurt.

Tonya only shrugged like she was used to their fighting.

Jesse stumbled away. "You guys should form a new band and see how that goes. Come on, baby, let's lie down in the stream." He motioned for the woman to follow his lead.

My body told me to run and hide. Ideally, I would have taken action rather than recoiling. I stood there, stiff and unable to help in any way. I was a young, useless girl who feared a man's wrath.

The tall dark woman rose and followed Jesse like a devoted puppy.

Betsy and Thomas sat in the lawn chairs, defeated.

"How long has he been drinking?" Keith asked.

"Since you left. He saw the bus and started drinking. The more he drank, the angrier he seemed," Betsy informed us.

"Yeah, he's a mean drunk," Mason said.

Everyone sat down in sorrow.

I picked up my shoulders and put one foot in front of the other. My body was tense. I tried to seem unaffected by the yelling. Fawn curled up at my feet with her ears standing straight up.

Thomas seemed on edge, while Betsy was beaming. She was probably happy she learned something new to gossip about.

The band bowed their heads. I was not against drugs or alcohol, but addiction was entirely different. I had obscure memories of my dad before he left, and he was similar to Jesse. Fortunately, my mind blocked those harmful recollections from rising to the surface, and I was too young to remember much of it. I thought that rockstars were supposed to be happy. They had life made. What was there to complain about?

"Is it the age-old tale of a rockstar who has a drug and drinking problem?" Darren questioned. I wasn't exactly sure what Darren was referring to.

"No, it's different. He has had this problem since we were teens. Fame just made it worse. Jesse hides from his demons by drinking or making music. When he can't get his way, he throws fits. He grows more irritable and lonelier with each tour we go on," Keith said.

They were saying that Jesse Young, the one that was a rockstar, the one every girl wanted to be with and every boy wanted to grow up to be, had a real problem. It had to be a mistake. I couldn't believe it was true. I convinced myself that maybe Jesse was just having a rough day, and it was an isolated event. There was no way someone as talented as him would be so violent.

"It's getting harder to take care of him. It's difficult seeing your best friend dig their grave," Keith said with a sigh.

"I joined the band because Jesse thought the British invasion would wipe out his band, so his solution was having a Brit join them. I was honored to stand as a woman and be equal to these guys. After a while I wasn't. Jesse only cared if he survived the next day, and he especially didn't value my opinion. It's not worth speaking out. Keith fights with him all the time, and it goes nowhere."

It was complicated. Hearing that your idols were ordinary people with issues was freeing and simultaneously terrifying. Darren's hand was bunched up in a fist by his side. If music was our God, how could he let the greats suffer? They said money and talent do not mean you will live a comfortable and happy life. Every magazine showed their luxurious mansions, yachts, and vacations. It didn't make any sense. Yes, sometimes there were tabloids about rockstar's divorces and drama, but I figured it was for publicity's sake. Drama made things more interesting. The first rule of writing was that there was no story without conflict.

"This is too heavy for a group of kids like you to carry. You are fans. Do you want to hear a couple of our songs? Our instruments are in the back. Then I will drive you into town," Mason said.

"I would like that." Music was my medicine. Although it was not a cure, it would help.

The band carried their instruments to the grassy area by the grill. Since there was no electricity, they had to improvise. Keith had a less intricate set of drums, Tonya had an acoustic guitar, and Mason had a Bauer Portable Mignon.

We sat in the cold and dewy grass across from them.

Keith counted them off with his wooden drumsticks. "One, two, three."

They began playing their top song "Bright." The tune was a love song with deep drumbeats and an electric feel. Without the bass and keyboard, it was a soft song. I felt like I was back in the park with James dancing around and throwing pennies into people's hats. There were no bells and whistles. It was back down to the basics. I was comfortable and in my element, so I moved to the music.

"May I have this dance?" Darren asked with a chuckle.

I took his hand and danced like I was a little girl again. I didn't need to lie about who I was. I could just exist with the music.

Betsy and Thomas danced next to us. They fumbled around, and Thomas stepped on Betsy's toes. She shrieked. "Stop being such a doofus. Watch where you put your feet!"

I minded my business by resting my head on Darren's chest and looking at the stars. He didn't try quick movements with his feet or popular dances like Thomas did. Instead, he held me as we moved our bodies back and forth.

The airstream's door swung open. "If you are going to play my song, then you need someone to sing the lyrics," Jesse said.

Fawn's head jolted up at the sound of Jesse's voice.

"You need to see that I am right in front of you. It's always been me. We are like fire when we ignite, baby together, we are bright," he harmonized the chorus.

He sang the rest of the song clearly as he took the lead. His gritty voice made the song go from gushy to rock. I thought the instruments made the song, but after hearing it live like that, I learned it was Jesse's voice. When the song came to an end, I rose onto my tippy toes to give Darren a kiss. His kisses were gentle and left me always wanting more.

Keith stopped playing and yelled, "Hey! You said you could play the drums. Why don't you come and play with the one and only Jesse Young and the Matches?"

"I don't know… I am not a professional like you guys," Darren said, timid.

Darren was being modest. He'd learned so much over the years, even though he wasn't a professional. If his dad had let him practice more, he could be something. He knew how to read music and could replicate a song's beat after one single listen. He had a talent, and most people would want to use that aptitude for money and fame. Darren, on the other hand, desired to use it to teach. I understood his need to inform others. I wanted to use my voice to critique music and reveal the truth. Whatever the truth really was.

"Darren, you may not be a rockstar yet, but you should play. Go learn how to become one," I said as I pushed Darren toward the band. He deserved to feel validated for his work.

"Fine. No promises it won't sound awful."

Darren sat on Keith's throne. It took him a minute to get comfortable. Using someone else's drums was like getting used to a different car. Drums had universal controls for the most part, along with small details that you had to use to pick up on.

"Hey, Jesse, this kid was singing a song he made from library sheet music. It's excellent. You should play it," he said, holding Darren's shoulder.

Darren inhaled and raised the sticks into the starry night. His hands began to fall until they suddenly stopped mid-air above his head. "Penny, you need to sing it for this to work. You are the one who made me go to the library. You already sang it once. It is only right."

## Chapter Sixteen
## Rocking Revolt

*Song: A Song For You—Donny Hathaway*
*April 4th, 1966*

Jesse studied me. "You can sing?"

"I can sing, but it's nothing special," I said.

Jesse stroked his mustache while he was thinking. "We should sing it together."

I couldn't believe it. I was going to sing with Jesse Young. His voice was the one I grew up listening to on the radio. I bought his first album with my tooth fairy money.

***Harold Hayes: You bought their album with your tooth fairy money?***

***Penny: It is a fun little story. I guess I can mention it.***

During a family yard sale, I bit into a chicken leg, and when I looked down, my tooth was stuck in the meat. I skipped into the carport and tapped James on the back. When he turned around, I held up the chicken leg as if I were holding a trophy. It took him a while to understand what I was showing him because he was negotiating the price of some old fishing gear with a man. My mom carefully removed the tooth from the drumstick, cleaned it, and helped me place it under my pillow when I went to bed.

The next day, I found two dollars and some change under the chilled side of my pillow. James asked me what I wanted to use the money for.

"Can we go to the record store Rocking Revolt?" I asked him. I had walked past the store before and saw the neon lights in the window.

"Sure. I think it's on Seventh and Main Street."

Rocking Revolt had endless crates of vinyl records to choose from. They carried popular bands to local up-and-coming artists. They had a color-changing jukebox in the corner of the store where you could request songs, three sound-listening booths, and globe lights hanging off the ceiling.

James and I were searching for an album we did not know of and amazed us. As we scanned through each album, one caught my eye. The cover depicted a man with tattoos and a dark, shaggy haircut sitting on a diving board with his boots hanging just above the water. A darker-skinned man with big hair behind him was preparing to push the other man into the pool. A blonde woman stood to the left of the diving board, holding an orange bass fender. On the right side of the board was a soft, curly-haired man pressing his fingers down on a keyboard. The chlorine water reflected their silhouettes, forming quite a breathtaking scene.

James detected that I was stunned by the image. He took the album out of my hands and flipped it over. On the back of the album was a picture of all their instruments thrown into the water. They had five songs on each side. The album was called, "Dive In."

"What do you think? The cover is cool," I said, looking for James's approval.

"I don't know. We should listen to it first."

James took me over to one of the listening booths. I sat criss cross applesauce on the fuzzy rug. He pulled the record from its protective sleeve and placed it onto the turntable. The first song was the same as the album's name. "Dive In" was a fun summery song. The chorus sang:

*"It's hotter than hell*
*There's nothing to do.*
*Darling, you might as well.*

*Dive into the blue."*

The rest of the tracks on the album had more experimental elements. I tugged on the shaggy carpet while I listened. "Sandy" was the second song on the A-side. It was a slower melody about heartbreak and wanting a simple life. "Catching a Cloud" contained a fascinating drum solo. "Sunrays Burn" was an intense song with loud bass chords. The lyrics held anger in them. It was about having a good time but being left with a sunburn that wouldn't go away. It was silly and nothing like anything I heard before.

As I sat and listened to the album, James inspected the cover in more detail. By the time we reached the B side of the record, I was smiling from ear to ear. It was the ideal album to buy with my tooth fairy money.

"Well, what's the verdict?" James asked.

"I will take it," I said as a little bit of saliva shot out from where my front tooth used to be.

The man at the front counter was wearing a tie-dye shirt. His hair was longer than mine, and he wore round, golden-framed glasses.

I jumped up to place the record on the counter.

"Right on. We just got this album in stock. The main singer, Jesse, and his friends used to live here in Butterfield when they were kids. I think Jesse Young and the Matches are going to become huge," the man claimed.

James winked at me when he said, "My daughter has good taste."

Then, James handed the man my tooth fairy money. He counted out the coins and put them in the register.

"Do you nice folks need a bag?"

"No, I think we are okay," James said, because he

knew I wanted people to see me with the album.

I was proud that my missing tooth funded my first record. I strolled down the sidewalk with a black hole in my mouth and the album facing toward any passing cars. The bright aqua water on the cover shimmered in people's side mirrors.

James held my other hand until we got back to his truck, ready to take it home and give it another listen.

## Chapter Seventeen
## Pitiful Peaches

*Song: Dance with Me—Orleans*
*11:30 PM*

Jesse ran to the airstream to get paper and a pen. When he returned, he had me write the lyrics in his notebook.

Darren wanted me to write it because his handwriting was ineligible.

Even though he wanted me to, I was worried the band would associate me with the song and not Darren.

Jesse let me sing it by myself for the first time so he would understand how the tune sounded. It was difficult to get started and sing the first word. My voice quivered a lot as I sang.

Jesse simply nodded along, memorizing the words.

The second time, Darren played the drums while Keith watched him. My high-pitched, uneasy voice and Jesse's gravel voice sounded good. Our voices were so different that they complimented each other.

Keith was admiring Darren's drum solo. The sheet music, combined with Darren's creativity, was less than forty seconds long, but it had something to it. It could be a catchy commercial song or jingle for selling peaches.

Jesse saw something else for its future. He started pacing while chewing on the end of the pen he held in his hand. He mumbled the lyrics under his breath like he was analyzing a poem in English class.

"What is he doing?" I whispered to Keith.

"It looks like you all are lucky. You got to see the real Jesse Young, and now you get to see how he writes songs."

Darren and I watched as he started scribbling and crossing out words.

"This might take a while," Tonya admitted as she lay on the wet grass, pulling her skirt down before it peaked up.

"How long is it going to take?" Betsy probed.

"I don't know. Depends on how inspired he gets," Mason said.

Jesse had a fascinating writing process. He would walk back and forth, humming the tune repeatedly, adding lines when he came up with something. I couldn't imagine what he was adding to Darren's song and how he would feel about it. I motioned for Darren to sit in the grass with me again. "What do you think he's doing to your song?"

"I don't care what he does with it, Copper. Jesse Young likes my song. That's enough for me."

I nodded, understanding how he felt. Singing with Jesse was the single most exciting thing I had done other than going to a concert with James. Being around someone who could explode any second was riveting. Jesse could make anyone feel special if he wanted to. The Matches, Thomas, Betsy, Darren, and I lay on the turf waiting to be called upon.

"Is this the way he has always made songs?" Darren asked.

"No. The first album we made together was when he valued other people's opinions. It didn't sell many copies, though. Not a lot of people even know about it," Keith confessed.

"Dive in was the first record I purchased for myself," I said, revisiting a memory of James.

"No way. That album only sold two hundred copies. We didn't even make back the money it took from ruining our instruments in the pool. Why we thought it was a good idea to throw them in, I don't know," Mason said.

"I am not kidding. I bought that record with my tooth fairy money."

Tonya laughed. "That is the Bee's Knees. I can't believe you did that. You must be really young then."

Everyone laughed and started pointing out the different constellations in the sky. It took me a minute to locate the big and little dipper. We joked about how aliens would abduct us, and no one would know where we went. I pretended I feared the green creatures to curl up with Darren. He wrapped his arm around me, and I played with the fabric of his shirt. Everything had happened so fast, but it was finally time for us to be peaceful.

My mind filled up with questions. Were my mom and James worried about where I was? Should I tell Darren I would be his girlfriend? What would happen to our friendship if I did? Would Darren be grounded? Was there a God in that night sky? And most importantly, would Jesse Young and The Matches be able to take care of Jesse's "problem" forever?

My brain did not have enough power to answer any of the questions. I was used to having time alone to think through my problems, but Jesse hated leaving any silence because silence meant a person had to deal with pain, and after seeing Jesse's outbreak, I thought he had a lot of built-up pain.

Jesse screamed, "*Tonya, Mason, Keith*, and *you guys* have to get over here right now!"

Darren shot up like a confetti cannon. He was ready to listen to his song be turned into a masterpiece.

Jesse was in his own world. He stuttered about how it was not perfected yet, and he needed the band to help him figure out how the music could complement his new lyrics. He was on a creative high.

"What do you got?" Keith questioned.

"Darry, you are the one who wrote it, right?" Jesse asked.

"Yeah, I am. Why?"

"Come here, read this, and tell me what you think first. Where are those peaches you guys stole? I'm going to need some if we keep working. I am starving."

I snuck a glance at the notebook paper as Darren read.

**Pitiful Peaches:**

*"When the peach flowers bloom*
*and the juice falls from your eyes*
*Remember that I don't bite*
*There is no need for goodbyes*
*One day, we will reunite*
*When they grow out of my tomb." –Jesse*
*"Pitiful Peaches are what I am to you.*
*We can swim at the beaches.*
*But my love is still true.*
*Pitiful Peaches keep me alive.*
*I would bleed for you.*
*Baby, we must survive.*
*Pitiful Peaches are sweet but tart.*
*Baby, baby, baby,*
*Please don't squeeze my heart.*
*Pitiful Peaches are what I am to you." –Darren*
*"When the peach flowers bloom*
*And you spit out the pit*
*Remember that I tried my best*
*Struggling is hard to admit*
*So please lay me to rest." –Jesse*

The chorus was repeated once more at the end. Jesse made Darren's simple love song into a compelling story about struggling with your inner self so much that you cannot love.

Darren turned to Jesse. "This is sensational. You turned my stupid tune into a sparkling gem. It has so many layers. These lyrics combined with Keith playing the drums, Mason's keyboarding, and Tonya's bass would be mind-blowing."

Darren was right. Jesse turned his sharp-edged rock and ran it through a tumbler. But it still needed to be polished. "You guys should all try to mess around with it and add something," I recommended.

Jesse scratched his head. "I guess that would be okay, but if I want to change something, don't get your panties in a bunch," he said as he whacked Keith on the back.

Keith whacked Jesse right back.

There was a reason Jesse Young and The Matches ended up in Moose Creek, of all places. Maybe we could help each other in ways I never dreamed of. Jesse and the band dove into the guitar case full of peaches, eating the juicy parts and spitting or throwing out their pits into the fire.

The night dragged on. The stars dimmed, and the air started to smell smokey. It was very faint. However, the atmosphere had changed. My clear breaths turned fogged as Jesse Young and The Matches perfected their new song, "Pitiful Peaches."

## Chapter Eighteen
## There's Always an End

*Song: Lonely People—America*
*1:00 AM*

The night was coming to a close as The Matches worked with Jesse to add their influence to the song. It reminded me of how "Dive In" sounded. Even though I was a fan of their newer album, it was different. Their latest album told one person's perspective, making it limited. The song was beautiful. It was how bands should work together. It was up for debate whether Jesse behaved so well because we were there or if the alcohol was wearing off. Nevertheless, I was happy everyone was getting along, and music was being made in my presence.

Ronny and the woman came out of the airstream to see what Jesse was doing. The woman kneeled to my level. "Isn't he wonderful?" she asked, enchanted by his talent.

"He definitely can be," I replied. I was unsure what to think after he threw the bottle at The Matches and us. He made Darren's song into a masterpiece. He couldn't be that bad if he was so great at making music.

Ronny said, "Once Jesse sobers up, he kicks the girls he parties with to the curb."

The woman huffed. "I knew he wouldn't keep me around very long, but a good time is a good time. He's not the first famous person I've been around."

I wouldn't be able to spend time with someone without getting attached. I was already struggling not to make any mistakes with Darren. I applauded the woman's ability to live without the thought of consequences, and how she surrounded herself with famous personalities.

My eyes drooped, and my vision became hazy. My arms were heavy spaghetti noodles. I wasn't used to staying up so late.

The woman was ushered and pushed out of the campground by Ronny.

"Well, safe travels, I guess. It was nice meeting you. Hey, I never caught your name," I said, yawning.

"Thanks, beautiful baby. I am off to find another band to follow around. I know one that's going on tour soon and they will let me stay with them. Have fun with these people. Don't get too stuck on them. There is much more out there. My name isn't important," she said, sashaying away.

I didn't know where she disappeared to. It wasn't like there were taxis in Moose Creek. I think that woman would have followed the wind if she could.

"You look like you need a nap," Betsy told me.

"I know I do, but I can't fall asleep here. I probably should go home. My mom and James will be worried sick."

Betsy nodded. "Yeah, at least your parents will be happy for you and won't mind. I don't know what Darren will do when he has to go home. I can just tell my parents I fell asleep at your house, and they won't question it. Or I could crawl through the window and pretend I was never gone."

The song needed to be polished more thoroughly, but the Matches were also losing steam. Eventually, Mason said, "Hey, Jesse, why don't we drop these kids off back in town and pick this back up tomorrow?"

"I don't want to quit, but we should take them home. They are starting to look bleak," he said with respect.

Keith looked at him as if he had turned into a different person, but the band began packing up their stuff so we could leave.

"Hey, Darry! Can I drive you and your friends home?" Jesse asked.

"Uh…"

"I can drive them. You can tag along. It's better if we take a back road. I would rather not run into that comically sad sheriff again," Mason said. I was thankful that Jesse was going to tag along, and it was good he wasn't driving after he drank.

"All right. Ron fetch Mason the keys."

Mason got into the driver's seat. Jesse called shotgun, so Tonya and Keith sat with us in the back. Thomas and Betsy rode in the row before us, leaving Fawn to lay on my shoes, bone tired. Darren looked so cute next to me. He was slouched over and his eyes had bags under them, but even then, he looked handsome.

That night proved Darren was worthy of being my boyfriend. He was kind and considerate, could play music, and didn't push my boundaries. I couldn't believe I had not seen Darren in that way before.

My only concern was if he would stay with me. How could we be together when I only saw him in the summer months? We were only going to be sophomores and had a couple more years of school. He would get bored and call it quits before next summer. It wasn't a good idea. Then, our friendship would be over for nothing. I also thought about James and how he was hurting. I knew that for James to feel better, we would have to go home. Even though we did not talk to each other as much as we used to, I owed him. I owed James everything.

I wrapped my arm under Darren's armpit to cuddle up to him. His irises dilated, forming big black holes. I scooted closer to him. The leather seats made the hair on the back of my calves stand up. I leaned my head onto his shoulder and rested my eyes. He followed my motion and tilted his head onto mine. His warm skin was comforting, and his shirt smelled like baby powder and cotton. I wanted to savor the moment. It would be the last time I would get to be romantic with him. I couldn't jeopardize our friendship. He would be a good boyfriend to someone, just not me. The next day, I would have tell him it was a mistake, that I wasn't ready for a boyfriend, and that I couldn't take the risk. Even if Darren disagreed, he would accept my decision because he wanted what was best for me.

Mason drove on the backroads until he crept into town. It was agreed that they would drop Thomas and Betsy off first. Betsy's parents would be upset if she came home late, so I was anxious to see if they would believe her story. The bus spilled into her driveway. Mason turned off the headlights to avoid being noticed.

Betsy smiled at us as she gathered her purse and belongings. "It was a treat to meet all of you! It's not every day that you get to meet someone famous. I doubt I will see you again, so thanks for the fun night! Don't forget to try out your new 8-track, Penny," she said before she kissed Thomas and told him she would see him soon.

The band waved their goodbyes as she snuck through the kitchen's window. I guess she chose the most straightforward way with no explanation. The window was low to the ground, and the way she hopped into the room was like she had done it hundreds of times before. I wondered if I was friends with Betsy because she reminded me of my sister. I never made the connection, but the image of her easily crawling in with messed up hair from her late-night adventures was similar. They both loved sneaking around because it gave them a rush. Betsy tugged the window down and gestured for us to go.

"That girl sure did talk a lot," Jesse said.

Thomas nodded. The car ride to Thomas's home was quiet. Thomas's parents didn't care where he was or what he did. As long as he made it home alive the next day, he was off the hook. Most of the time, when Thomas was home, he would stay at Darren's house because he didn't have much at home to look forward to. Since I only visited in the summer, I missed out on those moments. I couldn't imagine Thomas, Betsy, or even Darren wearing winter coats surrounding a Christmas tree or worrying about a big school project. The letters we sent back and forth throughout the holidays could only hold so much detail and perspective.

Thomas nonchalantly got out of the bus. "See you around." He slammed the bus closed, not anxious about the noise or getting in trouble. He opened his parents' unlocked door and closed it, walking into nothing.

My grip on Darren's arm tightened.

Mason started coughing. "I don't know why, but it's smokey out there," he said. Mason tried driving through the heavy fog. It was impossible to see clearly. The closer we got to my grandma's cabin, the thicker it got.

"What do you think is going on?" Tonya asked.

"I'm not sure. Maybe someone's barn caught on fire, or a campfire got out of hand," I said. Small fires weren't uncommon in the dry months. It was only June though, which was early in the season for forest fires to form.

We covered our mouths and noses with the collars of our shirts. It wasn't good to breathe in that much smoke.

Jesse rolled up the window to avoid inhaling more polluted air. The bus turned onto my street, and we saw the flames—the bright orange monster of a flame. Sheriff

Douglas's car, a fire truck, and an ambulance were sitting in front of my grandma's blazing cabin.

## Chapter Nineteen
## Burn it Down

*Song: Sailing—Rod Stewart*
*1:35 AM*

I shifted my body forward. I couldn't comprehend the smoking ceiling falling to the ground. My grandma's cabin, which I went to every summer, was gone. The former house full of my grandma's secret junk was completely engulfed in flames. My jaw fell when Darren put his hand on my back. He rubbed his fingers in tiny circles, reassuring me that everything would be okay, even though he didn't know what was happening. Darren was sweet like that; he knew when to step up and when to back down.

I didn't know where my mom or James were. I hoped that everyone was safe. James used to joke about setting a match to his mother's hoarding house, but it was just a joke. Some sort of freak accident had to have happened. I thought that maybe he accidentally didn't put out his cigarette correctly, or perhaps something electrical caught fire. Unfortunately, my grandma's collection was the perfect fuel for a fire. Her piles of clothes and books left against the cabin walls made for better kindling than the house itself.

"Let me out!" I screamed.

When I jumped out of the bus, I shoved Fawn's leash into Darren's grasp. I knew she would be in good hands with Darren. Sheriff Douglas would know who I was; he would recognize the bus, and we would be in trouble. All that mattered to me was my mom and James's safety.

I ran up to the blue and red lights with enfeeblement. Sheriff Douglas stood tall, his face conveying wrinkles of seriousness. When he became aware of me, he shook his head back and forth. "Young lady, what are you doing here? Haven't I seen you enough tonight?" he said with a grimace.

"What happened?" I gasped.

"That is confidential information for family members of the residence only. Please go back to your campground."

"You don't understand. That is my family's house," I said, asserting myself.

Sheriff Douglas kneaded his forehead. His eyes drooped with a predicament. "You are related to Mrs. Hartley and James Hartley?"

"Yes, I am James Hartley's daughter. Now tell me what happened!" I screeched.

Sheriff Douglas turned around to grab a note out of his glove department.

"What is this for?" I asked, wanting to see my family.

"Lying to a police officer is a federal crime. You are lucky I am not going to write you or your friends up for speeding as well. You will have a lot on your plate now. Go ahead and read it. This was taped to that red truck's window," Sheriff Douglas said, disheartened when he transferred the note into my hands. Inside the envelope contained the picture of me on my birthday, and the keys to the pickup. The crumpled letter read:

*Dear my beautiful wife and daughter,*

*I am sorry. This is not how I wanted this to go, but I couldn't do it anymore. This house taunts me. My mother is ill, and I cannot save her. I cannot live up to my dad's memory. I am a failure. I have failed in this life. I hope my Ma will take this as an opportunity to start something new instead of getting more stuff.*

*My job is unfulfilling. I love both of you, but I am*

*not flawless. I have done bad things, and I know you will be better off without me.*

*Penny, you are so bright and such a fantastic writer. I know you will become a music critic. Don't let this ruin your life.*

*April, find someone else to love in your lifetime. You are stronger than anyone I know, and you deserve the best. I love you. Good luck.*

*P.S. Give Penny my truck.*

My legs shook as I fell to the gravel. The edged pellets dug into my kneecaps, ripping the skin off. My head was full of pressure, and the light blinded me. How could James do that to us?

Darren's shoes crunched the gravel in front of me. "What's wrong?"

"James is dead," I said, making the situation confirmed with my words.

I pulled my legs into my chest, forming a ball. Firefighters were yelling at each other, but all I could think of was *James is dead, James is dead, James is dead. James. Is. Dead.*

Time froze and sped up at the same time. People talked to me. Nothing could break through my wall of consciousness. I think the Matches and Jesse held me while I cried, but I don't know. Darren was there. I know that because he towered over me, trying to block me from seeing the firefighters bringing out James's unidentifiable body and putting it in the ambulance. I still saw it. I saw the outline of his familiar gut that I used to hug. I saw his long legs and how his face wasn't his anymore. His mustache was gone, along with his other recognizable features. The man that the firefighters were wheeling away was not James anymore.

"Mom, where is my mom? I need my mom," I stuttered, unsure if my words could be heard.

I stayed still, hoping James would come and bear hug me if I didn't move. He didn't because he was gone. Another person left me. The one person who I thought would always be there was gone.

I jumped up when a high-pitched scream rang into the smoke. My mom was the only person other than me who could scream like that. Adrenaline rushed through my veins. My heart pounded; my hands shook. I had a purpose. I brushed off the bloody rocks stuck to my kneecaps and tried to find my mom in the chaos of the incident.

Darren and the gang kept a concerned eye on me as I staggered up.

The fire had been contained. Charcoal remains of the cabin were left. An outline, or ghost of the building structure, was all that prevailed from the fire. The ambulance wasn't there, which meant that James's body was gone too. I was grateful for the EMTs who took him away so I wouldn't have to be around his lifeless body. Some of our neighbors gathered around to figure out what was happening. People's faces sank with shock and horror at the tragedy.

Sheriff Douglas was talking to a woman with short, puffy blonde hair as he wrote information on his clipboard. The woman he was talking to was bouncing around as she wept. The situation required filling out more paperwork than Douglas was used to doing in an entire year. I knew Sheriff Douglas was genuinely upset about our loss by his glossed over eyes. The only time someone died in Moose Creek was retirees who lived long and fruitful lives. When the woman Douglas was talking to turned around to look at the house, I knew it was Momma.

I dashed toward her, collapsing in her arms. She held my head on her warm chest, running her fingers through my more intact curls as we both sobbed until our lungs were too tired to pump air, and we sounded like wisps in the wind.

CHAYLEE McCLEESE

# Part Three

## Chapter Twenty
## Are you there, God? It's me, Penny

*Song: Jackie Blue—The Ozark Mountain Daredevils*
*June 27th, 1975*

We stayed at Darren's house that night, though I don't remember how we got there. I couldn't sleep despite being exhausted. My body was ready for anything. Every slight noise made me twitch. I lay on the Lawrence's yellow couch, holding my mom while Fawn lay on the floor.

Even though Fawn was born in Darren's house, she was uncomfortable staying overnight in a place she wasn't used to. Her eyes had goop in the corners, making her look older and unrested. I scooped away the hardened crust while she turned away from me, looking for James.

"He's not here, girl. He's not coming back," I said.

Despite the situation, Gabriel would not let Darren stay with us. Gabriel was more afraid of our relationship than the fact that James died.

I wondered what Darren was doing. Did he sleep peacefully while I laid in his basement, afraid to get up? My mom finally fell asleep on me after hours of crying. I was done crying. Even if I tried, my eyes couldn't produce any more tears because they were as dry as the Atacama Desert.

I knew it was morning when I heard Gabriel rummaging through the kitchen cupboards. I pinched my eyelids shut as he peeked down the stairway, and his footsteps echoed back up the wooden steps. My legs were scratched and bruised. I itched the red bumps of scabs and bug bites with my fingernails.

Gabriel's lowered voice said, "I know you want to be there for her, but now is not the time. She needs to figure this out alone. You are too young to be getting into a serious relationship!"

"I will do what I want. Penny needs me, and don't act like this isn't about you wanting me to be focused on taking care of your kids."

"Death is not easy, son. She won't be herself. Don't make this about your siblings or me. This is about you. Not to mention that you were out all night with her! I am not stupid. I know what teenagers do alone."

"You don't know anything about me or what I do!" Darren yelled.

"Be quiet. You'll wake the poor girl up," Gabriel said.

Darren huffed as he checked on me.

I compressed my eyelids together harder. I needed to sleep. At least then, I wouldn't have to deal with everything. Darren's family used to adore me. I helped around the house, got Darren to be more involved with his siblings, and was polite. All of a sudden, his dad didn't like me because I lost someone. Things were so screwed up.

After Darren left, I thought about the day before. I thought about dancing with him as Jesse Young and the Matches played. I thought about how alive I felt. But everything had changed. I was a zombie, barely awake. James died. It had only been one night since the cabin fell to the ground. It had to be a dream. All of it couldn't be real. My mind drifted into a deep slumber, praying that I wasn't in real life. *Please be fantasy*, I begged.

****

When I woke, it was time to take action. Even

after sleeping for hours, I was not well rested. Darren made me a bowl of peaches and cream. I gnawed on the edges of the mushy peach slices, but I couldn't bring myself to eat them. When someone dies, everyone around you caters to you. Lots of people brought us food. I wanted to be left alone. Instead, I was presented with gifts and sweets when I couldn't stomach eating a single peach slice.

I sat at Lawrence's unusually long dining table, which typically held their nine-person family. Gabriel and his wife, Susan, sat on one end while my mother and I sat on the other. Gabriel clasped his hands together on the surface of the counter. Darren's siblings were nowhere to be seen. I assumed they sent the children to the park or a friend's house while dealing with my family's circumstances.

"Girls, I am sorry for your loss. I expect your feelings to be raw. Please do not hesitate to stop me at any time. You may stay as long as you need. We have gathered to talk about the funeral arrangements." Due to the size of Moose Creek, Gabriel was the town's preacher, marriage officiant, and funeral director.

My mother nodded her head. He discussed different funeral packages and their costs. He sounded like he was selling us a new car. "The normal service and burial costs five hundred dollars. You will have to decide between cremation and burial. If you do not want his body cremated, we will have to discuss casket models and their prices…"

Gabriel's speech lasted a lifetime. By the end of his tangent, I wanted to scream. We'd just lost someone, and Gabriel was bombarding us with too much information. Without James, we couldn't even afford a candy bar, let alone five hundred dollars. We would have to use all of our savings to pay for the cost of his funeral.

I wanted to write James's obituary, but there wasn't any way to pay for it either. We could only afford the bare minimum.

I put my hand out to stop him from speaking. Susan was staring at us with a proud, tight lip. Momma looked disoriented. "We want your cheapest funeral service, and we want him cremated so we can take him to the cemetery in Butterfield. We will give you the pedal boat if you give us a discount. Now stop talking. You are upsetting my momma," I said, rising from the table and walking my momma back to the basement.

James would have wanted to be put in a fancy wooden box six feet under. I couldn't care about what he wanted because I knew Momma, and I couldn't bare seeing his body the way it was. I needed to keep the image of James before he died in my mind if I were going to survive with poise. "I need to go outside to get some fresh air," I informed Darren. I had to leave his house. It was claustrophobic, and nothing felt like home.

There was nowhere to go anymore, so I chose to sit on Darren's front porch, where I got Fawn many years ago. I refused to look down the street at the cabin's remains. It had to be midday; the sunshine touched my bare skin, but I was still cold. The sun's power to vitalize me had vanished, along with my level head.

Shortly after, Darren followed me onto the porch.

"Where are your siblings? Whenever I am here, they normally jump around and cause chaos. It's quiet today. Almost too quiet."

"My dad sent them to fulfill the duties of the church. They are cleaning up the chapel for the funeral."

"Oh. That makes sense," I said, in a muddle.

"I am sorry about my dad. He has done this for so long that I think he has become insensitive to death. To him, it is just another day on the job," Darren said, sitting next to me.

"It's fine. I know he doesn't want us here anyway. He thinks I will corrupt you. Maybe he is right," I snapped.

"Copper, he's wrong. I don't care what my father wants or thinks. I will be there for you through thick and thin," Darren responded.

I'd thought James would be there for us, but he left. I wanted to believe Darren would stay and be there for me through everything. James was there for years, and yet I was alone and fatherless. People didn't care about me, James, or Momma. They only wanted to drain our pockets and suck the marrow out of our bones.

"I don't know anymore," I said, putting my hands over my eyes.

*Are you there, God? It's me, Penny. At this point, I don't believe you are real.*

## Chapter Twenty-One
## The Funeral

*Song: A Working Class Hero—John Lennon*
*June 30th, 1975*

I pulled down the tight and itchy fabric on Susan's black dress that I'd borrowed. Combing my messy hair with my fingers made me look ridiculous. Black clothes made me look plain. I had to wear the color of death because it was time to say goodbye to James … or what was left of him.

Susan and Darren were in charge of inviting everyone to the funeral. My grandma refused to come. She said that no son of hers would do such a thing. I didn't know if she was talking about him burning her house down or leaving us like he did. I saw it as one less upset person we had to deal with. She would blame my mom anyway. Without James connecting us to my grandma, I doubted she would want us around. James kept everyone together. My grandma wouldn't be out of much from the fire. She had a lot of stuff, but it wasn't worth anything. I'd had a lot of things in the bedroom when the house crumbled. Pictures of the summer, clothes I'd cherished, and ceramics I'd made. My grandma had her house back in Butterfield, and due to the circumstances, she would receive an extensive insurance check for the lost cabin.

My sister couldn't get a flight home in time, so she didn't attend either. A few townsfolk had already sent in RSVPs, and my friends stayed home from camp to support me.

Susan suggested that we wait to have the funeral for a while, because the number of guests was limited. Postponing the funeral would only prolong the inevitable.

It was time, and if people didn't want to clear their schedules to come, neither would Momma and me.

Darren's reflection appeared behind me in the mirror. "Are you ready for today?"

"Not really."

"Well, I have a surprise for you. Jesse Young and The Matches agreed to come to the funeral," Darren said, trying to lighten the mood.

"That's nice of them. I figured they would be out of town by now." It was surprising to hear that James's favorite band would be at his funeral. I wish he could have met them before he passed away. Perhaps he would still be here if he saw that even famous people could be broken. I struggled not to think about what would have happened if... If I was there. If I'd stayed in the cabin. If I didn't kiss Darren. If. I should have gone home earlier the night he died. I should have done so many things differently. If I could go back … I would. Gabriel told me that thinking about what-ifs didn't help, and yet I asked myself it over and over.

The funeral was held in the local church. I pictured getting married at the Moose Creek church. It had rainbow-colored stained-glass windows, long wooden church pews, and gray carpet that you could dig your toe into while you listened to extended services. It held a sentimental place in my heart. My family rarely attended church, but I occasionally frequented the building after becoming friends with Darren, and something about being in the building made me at ease.

The church was only a couple blocks from the Lawrence's house, so we walked to the chapel. Darren held my body up while I held my mother. I was moody, yet Darren stayed a constant in my life. He brushed off my indecisiveness while staying calm and collected. Our black attire contrasted with the bright hues of summertime. My mother's dark, pellucid train waved as we marched to God's doors.

Gabriel wanted us to get to the church a couple of hours before the ceremony to prepare the tiny details. When we arrived, flowers, cookies, and other goodies were already displayed on the table by the entrance. On an average day, Darren would have devoured the table. Rather than feeding his sweet tooth, he pointed them out by saying, "Isn't that nice?"

I nodded. Gifts were lovely, but food could not return someone from the dead. My momma needed me to be strong for her that day.

When Betsy arrived, she helped me put marigolds around the podium on which James's ashes were presented in a red urn. The red urn caught my eye. I had seen it before. I stared at the container, tracing my memories back to my grandma's wrinkled hands painting it. She didn't show up, so she had sent her condolences in the only way she knew how: stuff. Although she treated us so poorly, I hoped she would be okay.

I snuck Gabriel the note I wanted him to say during the service and ensured everything was going well. The plan was what kept me sane and was how I dealt with the numbness inside of me. Flowers, check. Speech, check. Check on Momma, check. Guest book? I made Susan add a guest book to the front so people could sign their names and write down their favorite memories about James. Check.

People began to arrive a quarter before the scheduled service. I watched them from behind a privacy curtain. Gabriel said there was no shame in sitting in the secluded area. I knew I should have been the one sitting in the front row displaying my grief so that others would follow. I couldn't bring myself to put my emotions out there. The curtain was cowardly, but it was what I needed.

Betsy, Thomas, and Zach weren't allowed to sit with me because of the restricted number of seats behind the curtain. They sat in the pews after they chatted with me for a while. Some people knew exactly what to say when someone dies, but my friends didn't. They did their best, and that was all I could ask of them.

I couldn't cry or have a sudden outburst, weep, or talk about my memories with James. I couldn't feel the sadness I wanted because I wasn't ready to. My posture was magnificent because I was hardened.

There were even fewer people than I expected. Jesse Young and the Matches had yet to show their faces, but the show had to go on. Gabriel approached the podium, while straightening out his tie. "Thank you to those who have come. Today, we are celebrating the life of James Hartley. James Hartley was a kind and hardworking man. He was born and raised in Moose Creek. He moved to Butterfield when he was a teenager. He worked at a small lumber mill to provide for his family. He is survived by his wife, April Hartley, mother, Harriet Hartley, and his stepdaughters, Penelope Hartley and Breanna Hartley."

Gabriel made James sound like your ordinary run-of-the-muck middle-aged man. He didn't talk about how he would lend someone the shirt off his back or his love for music. James was simplified to a man who died and worked.

My momma held a handkerchief that she blew her nose into. Darren sat beside me, allowing me to be tranquil. Gabriel went on a tangent about some bible verse that I was unsure related to the situation. Still, his target audience ate up his preaching, sometimes adding an "amen" after a sentence or phrase he spoke.

"Penelope Hartley wanted me to say that he

brought happiness into her mom's life that she couldn't give her and that he was the best dad figure she had. She is going to miss him because she already does," Gabriel said, paraphrasing from my detailed note. He turned my long and beautiful tribute into a blurb. I wanted to scream, but instead, I squeezed Darren's hand as hard as I could. I let out all of the tension into it, and all he did was gently squeeze my hand back in acceptance.

Warm light seeped in from the outside world when Jesse Young and the Matches stumbled in. My anger disappeared at the sight of them.

"Sorry! I know we are late. Go on!" Jesse drunkenly exclaimed in a black tux as he fumbled into the last row.

Keith grabbed him by the collar to push him into the seat. Keith wore a nice dark gray suit tailored for his long legs. It was the darkest color I had ever seen him pictured in. The Matches had clumpy bags under their eyes. I looked worse, but what did it matter? I could hide. They were always in the public eye.

Tonya and Mason politely smiled at the other guests.

Whispers still traveled through groups about who they were and what they were doing there. I proudly pointed them out to my momma. Even though she wasn't as big of a fan as James and I were, she liked Jesse Young and The Matches' music. She hardly acknowledged their attendance. Her eyes remained on the front of the chapel, while she sniffled and wailed.

As the service continued, the guests were asked if they wanted to share something about James. One man stood up and talked about how James was a fine man who helped him mow his grass every summer. A woman described how James complimented her hair whenever my momma cut her hair for her. No one said anything too emotional or descriptive because no one wanted to endure the weight.

Betsy looked toward the curtain before she rose and said, "James was a great father. Every summer, he cared for us girls by cooking us fish or checking in on us to make sure we were having a good time." She patted her eyes with a tissue and sat down as fast as she stood up.

I wished I could have ran out and thanked her.

Thomas followed his girlfriend's lead by saying, "James always made me laugh and got me out of my shell."

Zach partly stood, adding, "He was great at guiding me as I got older." I was shocked by Zach's comment. Even though Zach was a part of our friend group, he wasn't as around as my other friends. He stayed with his cousins most summers, and that summer he went to camp. It was interesting to think about all the different things James did that I wasn't aware of. I was honored to have such caring summer friends. We might not have seen each other during the school year. However, they knew me better than most people did.

"Does anyone else want to share something before the service ends?" Gabriel asked.

"Actually, I do," Jesse hollered.

"Of course. Go right ahead. This is an open space," Gabriel said, tapping his Oxfords on the floor.

"I didn't know this Jake you are talking about. I know his daughter, though. I don't know where she is. Penny! Where are you?" he said, looking through all the pews. "Anyway, his daughter is this awesome young girl, and it's so awful that Jake committed suicide. Don't you say that people who do that go to hell?"

Betsy gasped with horror. I felt like I was hyperventilating. My momma sobbed harder. I couldn't catch my breath because it was running away from me. How could Jesse announce to the entire town that James committed suicide? They didn't need to know that James left us on purpose. When people knew, they looked at us with depressing and pitiful eyes. Jesse dragged me onto a stage I didn't want to be on and put me in the spotlight.

"Well, biblically speaking, in most cases, people who commit suicide do not go to heaven because they are going against God's plan. I would happily answer any questions you may have after the service," Gabriel said.

That was proof that James would not go to heaven. Proof that James's demons had won. If there were a God who didn't love James for who he was, then I would rather go to hell than have a relationship with him. Jesse, on the other hand, was barbaric. I couldn't believe he would do that to me. He could write a beautiful song about struggling yet see it as a joke. I wanted to hit him, tear up his albums, or run out of the church. What was wrong with people?

Once the service was over, Gabriel pulled the curtain away from us. My friends greeted me by giving me gentle pats on the back, asking if I needed anything, and waiting for me to break down.

I stood tall, going through the motions.

Quiet voices confabulated, "Suicide? Is that how he died?"

Jesse lay passed out on one of the pews, snoring. His feet hung off the edge, and drool dribbled down his chin onto his expensive attire.

Keith tried kicking Jesse awake, but Jesse did not open his eyelids. He made a loud, snoring growl, falling into his slumber deeper.

Tonya and Mason were eating chocolate chip cookies from the table.

"There you are. We are so sorry for your loss.

Jesse, you know how he gets… Darren invited us, and I wanted to let you know that if you need anything, you are welcome to reach out," Tonya said as she clutched my body. It was nice to hear another woman's voice since men dominated most of the conversations that day.

I didn't know how Jesse got. I wanted to believe he was a good person because he was a good artist. Yet his impromptu speech was repulsive.

"We mean it, kid. You helped us out, and we owe you. Call us anytime," Mason said, handing me a ripped page of Jesse's book with a number on it in Tonya's handwriting.

"Sure. Thanks," I said as I pushed past them, unwilling to talk to them any longer.

Darren met me outside. Before I could say anything, he kissed me.

I slipped into our rhythm and let the kiss go on a little too long. "I don't think I can cry anymore. I must be really messed up. Tomorrow, we leave back to Butterfield, and there is no reason you should put your life on hold for me," I admitted.

"Penny, you know that isn't true. After everything my dad has pulled, I know I can't stay here much longer. I promise I am going to be with you. We need each other."

I pushed him away from me with all the strength I had left in my body. "No, Darren. I am going to go home, and things will be different now. You can't be my boyfriend. It couldn't work."

His eyes glistened. "Please don't shut down. It's okay to be broken. You just lost someone close to you. We will make this work."

"I said no. You are just like your dad. You think you are helping, but you aren't!" I screamed, knowing that it would make him leave me alone.

Darren's dark hair swooped as he turned around, heading back into his father's church, arms raised in defense. He said, "You are angry now, and I, of all people, get that, but it doesn't mean you need to lash out. I will give you time. Send me a letter when you get back home."

****

Betsy's parents offered to let us stay in their guest bedroom for the night. I didn't want to be at Darren's after the funeral. Seeing him would make me regret my decisions, and I couldn't change my mind before I left. Plus, they owned my dream house. It was made in the 1800s and had gorgeous bay windows, a wrap-around porch, floral wallpaper, and a spiral staircase. Momma went to bed with Fawn early while Betsy and I sat in their attic. Betsy and I used to go up there to play with our dolls and stuffed animals.

"How are you feeling?" Betsy asked while staring into my soul.

"As good as I can be."

"I'm sorry. I don't know what to say to make it better. I will miss him a lot too. I couldn't imagine losing my dad, or anyone for that matter. I had to flush a goldfish once. What does it feel like?"

"Currently, I feel on edge. I feel ready to take action at any given moment. I'm not sad yet, and I'm scared that it makes me crazy."

Betsy stood up from the chaise next to the window. "Well, if you aren't hurting, we might as well spend your last night here wisely."

"I am pissed at Jesse. Other than that, I feel okay. How would we do that?"

"It's a girl's night! We haven't had the chance to have a sleepover all summer. We are long overdue for some makeovers, boy talk, fashion shows, and some good old TV."

Betsy dragged me into the bathroom, where we did each other's makeup. It took me a couple of tries to do hers with my shaking hands, but in the end, she looked pretty. Her auburn hair made her look bold in a stunning way. I gave her a darker shade of red lipstick and a smokey eye. She painted my face more subtly with pink lip gloss and tan eyeshadow. The little bit of makeup went a long way. It brought back some color to my face.

We went through her mother's closet like we used to and picked out some funky dresses to wear. Then, we walked down the attic's middle, sashaying like we were runway models. I couldn't help but laugh when Betsy posed and blew me kisses.

I wasn't sure if should have been enjoying life. James was dead, and I was prancing around like nothing happened. Who did I think I was? I should have been holding my mom or crying my eyes out, reminiscing about him. Despite my family's open wound, I was laughing. Something was wrong with me. I curled up again, petrified by the world.

Betsy asked, "Why don't we put on pajamas and watch television on the couch downstairs?"

"All right," I said.

We sank into the couch's cushions, mindlessly watching the random programs that were on. When the sun rose, I would have to leave Moose Creek early, without James and without saying goodbye to Darren, as a cold, empty body without a soul.

## Chapter Twenty-Two
## Drive

*Song: Landslide- Fleetwood Mac*
*March 7th, 1974*

James's ruby red 1951 Chevrolet 3100 pickup became mine. He'd loved that pickup with all his heart, and since I was fifteen, I could get my license soon. Before James passed away, I didn't think I would have a car of my own until I was older. I still remembered the first time he let me drive it.

***Harold Hayes: You should write this story too.***

***Penny: Don't you think people will get bored of me re-hashing the past?***

***Harold Hayes: Do I look bored to you?***

***Penny: No. I guess not.***

It was a warmer day in March. It was too cold to be outside and too sunny to stay locked up in the house. I wanted to prepare sprouts for the garden, but if I put them out, there was a chance they would freeze.

Instead, I focused on nursing James. He was in one of his funks, and I begged him to do something with me all week. Sometimes, it worked, but most of the time, I made no progress.

"Can you take me to the corner store? I need to get a few things," I asked him repeatedly.

He rolled over and said, "No. I'm tired. I'm going back to sleep."

I gave up and decided to read instead of harping on him.

Later that week, he rushed into the kitchen and said, "Grab your jacket. We are going on an adventure like you wanted."

When I pestered him to tell me what we would

do, he refused. I tied and fastened the laces of my ropers, grabbed my jean jacket with the puffy snowball collar, and headed out the door.

I went to get in the passenger side when he threw his keys at me and said, "Not today. You are going to drive."

"I can't drive! I don't know how." I felt panicked. What If I wrecked his pickup?

"That is exactly why you need to learn," James said, patting me on the back. He took my place on the passenger side and told me to get in.

I sat in front of the steering wheel, nervous but eager to learn.

"Learning to drive is similar to learning how to ride a bike. You just need to take it slow and easy. Go ahead and start her up."

I put the keys into the ignition and turned it forward. The truck rumbled, and the noise of it running made me jump a bit.

"Great! See, you've got this. Now, you must put her in reverse and back out of the driveway. You will want to keep your foot on the brake and ease off of it to move. Are you ready?"

"I think so."

I looked behind me like I saw James do every time he backed out of a parking space. I shifted the gear into reverse and released my foot from the break.

"Good, slow and steady."

The truck sped up too much, so my immediate reaction was to put my foot back down, but the vehicle stopped faster than I expected.

James was jerked forward. "Haha. Okay, okay, keep going. You're doing fine. When you hit the end of the pavement, start turning the wheel left," he said, motivating me to keep trying.

I took my time backing out of the driveway. Backing up was the hardest part. When we finally got on the road, I became more assured of my abilities.

"That was great. Now, why don't you drive us to the corner store?"

"The corner store is across town. Can I drive that far?" I asked, while hitting my finger on the wheel.

"I think you can. You are the one who wanted to go," he said, turning up the volume of the radio. Although I only drove twenty miles per hour, I felt like I was cruising down the highway. James cranked his window down and hung his arm into the breeze. I could see his smile out of the corner of my eye.

We practiced how to stop at stop signs, follow the speed limit, and how much to turn the steering wheel. I yanked the wheel too much, so James held onto the dash for safety. When we reached the corner store, things were going more smoothly.

James told me to run in and ask the cashier to put three dollars on pump number five.

I put the truck in park and dashed through the store to get him a bottle of root beer and myself a Peppo from the ice chest. He surprised me, so I returned the favor with the sodas.

James was pumping gas into the Chevy, tapping his boot on the concrete with a smile on his face.

I handed him the bottle.

"Thanks, I love you," he said as he popped off the top of the root beer.

That was the James I knew and loved. He was the most understanding and supportive person to me when he was present. On the way back to our house, he didn't correct my driving because he knew I could figure it out alone. We talked about our new music interests, his job, and how school was going for me.

"I am really proud of the woman you are becoming. You are smarter than I have ever been. I wasn't good at school like you are."

"I'm not that great. I just like to read and write. I have a B in my math class. Trust me, I am not a genius; I just pay attention and turn in my assignments."

"Yeah, when I was in high school, I left my homework crumpled up in my locker."

I laughed. "No wonder you didn't do very well."

James wasn't the best father in the world. When he got in his funks, he was irritable and hid from me, but we had fun on the days he pushed through. Sometimes, we fought over little things, like when I didn't help my mom with the dishes or when I was tired of his cranky remarks when he got off work. However, at the end of the day he was there for me.

I had so many people in my life who cared about me. James cared in a way that I wasn't sure I would survive without. I know now that he was preparing me for a time when he couldn't drive me around anymore. He might have known his fate before I realized he was hurting. In his death, he left me his prized possession. Driving helped James collect his thoughts, and he passed that opportunity on to me.

## Chapter Twenty-Three
## Butterfield

*Song: Born to Run—Bruce Springsteen*
*July 1st, 1975*

Leaving Moose Creek with nothing other than the clothes on our backs was weird. Typically, we left in the late August heat and had to pack up the back of the truck with all of our possessions and the newfound treasures we collected over the summer. Sweat would pour down our backs as we cranked the windows down to cool off. But it was July and only seventy-six degrees. I patted Fawn's confused head when she jumped in the back of the pick-up, not understanding why we were leaving so early.

"Thanks for letting us stay over. It helped a lot," I said, thanking Betsy.

"Not a problem! Please keep in touch and have a safe trip back." Betsy gave me a hug and waited until we were ready to leave.

She lingered around until I finally said, "Don't worry about me. I will be okay." I wasn't sure if I would be okay, but I didn't want her to fret.

"I can drive us home, Momma."

My mom did not argue like she had in the past. She didn't have much fight left, so she flung me the keys, and I drove around the familiar turns, finding solace in the yellow dotted line. I gripped the wheel tightly, thinking about how James's cracked hands glided from side to side. I missed him. We had to return to the home he built for us without him. It was surreal.

During the first week at home, I slept in my momma's room with her. My twin bed was too singular, and Momma's king was too vast for her tiny body. We only had each other, and we both didn't want to be alone. But Momma only got up to go to the bathroom and occasionally eat. It didn't take long before I couldn't stand being cooped up in James's house while Momma cried for hours on end. Our rent was due soon, and I knew I would have to be responsible to make up the money. Momma's haircut money paid the electric bill. If we wanted to survive on our own, we needed more income, since we spent most of our savings on the funeral. My parents weren't extremely transparent with their spending habits. Yet, it was obvious we were not rolling in cash. I kissed my momma's forehead, who was lying on the couch staring at the ceiling. Then I let Fawn go to the bathroom and drove to the grocery store.

The grocery store down the road from our house was a Grocery Outlet. It was a nice store that happened to be the place where my mom and James's love story started. Although Grocery Outlet was a chain store, this one was owned by a sweet couple. They liked to give back to the community by donating to the food bank, the animal shelter, and more.

I never had to work for something I wanted other than in school and needed to learn how to balance everything. I was determined to make a difference as James did. If working were anything like school, I knew I would be okay. I could memorize content, apply it to tests, and follow the rules to a T without criticizing my teachers or making their lives more difficult. The idea of having a summer job wasn't something new. I thought I would have at least a year or two before flipping burgers or scooping ice cream rather than sitting by the pool or messing around in Moose Creek. But it was a better time than any. It was better to be distracted than to be free with my thoughts.

I approached the register and asked the young

cashier, who looked miserable, if I could talk to the owners.

With her eyebrows raised, she ushered me into a back office.

The owner, Fernando, welcomed me in. “What can I do for you?” Fernando was a Hispanic man who came to our country to give his family a better life, and he did. He was kind and loved to talk to people. Every time I entered the store and he saw me, he would greet me and tell me about all the latest deals.

“Hi. My name is Penelope Hartley. I live down the street. I am reliable, hardworking, and friendly. If you give me a chance, I would be a fantastic worker,” I said, reaching out my hand for a shake. Introducing myself as Penelope and not Penny felt wrong, but it was my full name.

“Woah! That was a great pitch. Aren’t you a little young to be working?” he asked as he firmly took my hand.

“Please, Sir, I really need a job,” I said, crossing my fingers.

Fernando clapped his hands together. “Let’s see what I can do. Stay here.” I was numb in the grungy, hollow office, with only one desk and some cardboard boxes. Standing in the empty room reminded me of how desperate I looked.

Fernando’s wife returned from the stockroom with a red employee shirt bundled up in her grasp. His wife had tanned skin, naturally pink lips, wide eyes, and light brown hair pulled up into a ponytail that flipped back and forth as she worked. She was a hard worker. I saw her lots of times on the floor stocking products or talking to customers.

“My husband alerted me that a determined young girl needs a job, and I have this small employee uniform that is not getting used. Do you think it will fit?"

"Yes, does this mean I got the job? Thank you so much. I won't let you down," I said, giddy about the job opportunity. I hoped they didn't just hire me out of pity, but a job was a job, no matter how I got it.

My first week, I showed up to work on time, came in when other people called in sick, and put on a fake and friendly smile when each customer walked through the door. My childhood was over. I couldn't pretend to only care about books, Elvis, or gossiping with Betsy anymore. I saw how brutal life could be, and I needed something stable.

Every night after work, I tried to write a letter to Darren. I couldn't bring myself to actually write and finish the letter. Crumpled pieces of paper were balled up in the trash bin next to my desk. What would I tell him? We still can't be together. I was a cashier who didn't feel emotions. He deserved the best, and I couldn't give him much. I was broken. Gabriel was right all along.

I got into a consistent routine: get up at six in the morning, make breakfast, do the dishes, make sure Momma was still taking care of herself, feed Fawn, let Fawn out, get dressed, go to work, count money, smile at a customer, scan grocery items, break down boxes, come home, shower, eat dinner, let Fawn out again, check on Momma, get in bed with her, and do it all over again.

Life was repetitive until I got into the truck to head to work on the Fourth of July and heard the unbelievable through James's truck's speakers.

## Chapter Twenty-Four
## You're on the Radio

*Song: Fame—David Bowie*
*July 4th, 1975*

The Fourth of July was a day to celebrate our country, our freedoms, and our liberty. I might be free, but I was trapped in a cycle of grief.

I flipped my employee shirt over my head, shimmied on a pair of jeans, and drove to work like any other day. Even though James's truck was technically mine, I didn't change a thing about it. His fuzzy red dice still hung around the rearview mirror, the trash from his late-night snacks lay under the seat, his cigarette butts lay in the cupholder, and a manly odor lingered in the air.

As I turned into my parking spot under a tree for shade from the heat to keep the truck in mint condition, I moved the volume dial up. The station was untouched on 105.1 The ROCK! The man on the radio said smoothly, "Thank you for listening to 105.1 THE ROCK! Happy Fourth of July. Remember to light off fireworks, hang out with your friends, and listen to amazing music. Here is Jesse Young and the Matches' new single…"

I put the truck into park. I checked the time on my watch, which showed that I'd arrived at work early, leaving me time to spare. I turned the dial up a little farther, hoping that what was to come was what I thought it was.

The song started with the low hum of a guitar, then a steady beat of the drums. My hands fell to my lap because Darren's song was playing on the radio. Jesse's raspy voice sang the lyrics I saw him scribble down two weeks before. My first thought was, "Wow, this song is perfect." My eyes watered, and my jaw fell in awe. I understood the lyrics even more because I had a personal connection to them. I was enraptured for other people to hear Darren and Jesse's combined brilliance. I paused, waiting to hear the announcer say Darren's name or something about how the song came to be, but he didn't.

At the end of the track, the man exclaimed, "Woah, folks, Jesse Young really is a star. He wrote and recorded the track in less than a week. 'Pitiful Peaches' is climbing the charts, already placing in the Top Ten. Next, we have Aerosmith."

I hit the steering wheel with my palm in frustration. My hand stung with pain from my rash reaction, but I didn't care. Darren wrote that song, and Jesse was taking all the credit. I turned the entire radio off, tucked my hair behind my ears, and put on my customer service face because underneath I was pissed. The day dragged on and my anger rose.

After a long day at work, it was time for me to clock out. Out of habit, I bought a pack of sparklers to bring home. On the Fourth of July, I would bring a pack of sparklers to Darren's house and let his siblings run around the yard with them. Betsy, Thomas, and Zach would join us. Betsy would paint little designs of flags and stars on the kids' faces while we would get a kick out of watching them try to draw pictures in the air. They thought they were making beautiful artwork to celebrate our country, but all it did was form streaks of light in the sky as they clumsily drew. I wondered what they were doing without me.

When I got home, I heard faint whining and someone sniffling their nose. I knocked on Momma's bedroom. "Are you okay, Momma?"

"I am fine, Penny. Go away," she said as quiet as a mouse.

I opened the door and crawled into bed with her. I

pulled her and James's heavy brown comforter over my body and wrapped my arms around her. The weight of the blanket fell over my body and made me seep deeper into the mattress. Fawn was shaking in between us.

"She is scared of the fireworks," Momma said.

"I know the loud noises scare her. Momma, it's okay to cry."

Momma's short blonde hair was pulled up on top of her head, forming a messy knot. Her nose was red and blotchy, leaving raw skin under it. She must have been crying for a while.

"I miss him. He was everything to me, and now he is gone. I don't know how to live without him. Why wasn't I enough for him to stay?" she cried.

"I don't know," I said, curling my legs into her. I wish I had more answers for her, but I was lost.

Fireworks shot into the air and made loud explosions. We lay cuddled up together. Fawn's tiny body tremored, my momma's shoulders fell up and down as she cried, and I sobbed for the first time since the night James died. I despised seeing her that way. She didn't deserve to be a widow. I didn't think I had any more tears left, yet I turned into a sloppy, inconsistent waterfall. After draining all the water from my tear ducts, I stood up and said, "I bought some sparklers. Do you want to light them up in the backyard?"

"Not right now. I don't want to get up."

"Please, Momma."

Momma dreaded getting out of her safe chamber. Yet she gradually moved her legs to the side of the bed and rose, for me. I let Fawn run around freely. Instead of frolicking, she put her tail between her legs and hobbled beside me. I opened the pack of sparklers, grabbed some matches from the kitchen, and went to our carport.

My momma crossed her arms while I messed with

the matches. I hit the side of the box a couple of times to get the match lit. When it finally lit, an innocent streak of orange with an outline of blue appeared. Flames were dangerous when they got big enough. I could still see the cabin engulfed in flames as it crumbled to ashes, except the match I held in my hand was nothing like that. I placed the match at the end of the sparkler, and it started to simmer. Tiny sparks flew in every direction, beguiling me. I handed my momma one and lit another. Momma moved the sparkler around in weak tiny circles.

"Watch this," I said, strutting around and shaking the sparkler to form the letters J-A-M-E-S in the air. My stepdad's name shimmered and disappeared into the darkness.

Momma excitedly put her hands over her mouth in amazement. She tried to speak, but she choked back tears. She followed my lead, raised her sparkler, and wrote in the air I M-I-S-S Y-O-U.

We wrote to James in the air all the things we couldn't say out loud. Momma and I even wrote how angry we were that he left us the way he did. We drew hearts, the names of his favorite songs, memories we had with him, and scribbles of pain we held deep inside our chests. We went through every sparkler in the pack, and I finally felt like we would be okay. We would survive together one word at a time.

## Chapter Twenty-Five
## Phone Calls

*Song: Telephone Line—Electric Light Orchestra*
*July 5th, 1975*

I knew I had messed up with Darren when I pushed him away. Darren had been there for me invariably. I should have called or written to him when I got home from Moose Creek. I was troubled that it would be too late to make amends as friends or whatever else we were, but I had to try.

I dialed his number by putting my finger into the circular rotary of the green phone next to my bed. My mom was gone cutting a client's hair, so I didn't have to worry about her getting on the other line to listen in. When I was younger, I liked to listen to my sister's conversations on the phone with her friends. Sometimes, she would hear my breathing and yell, "Penny! Get off the phone and stop being such a creep." Now, I understand the desire for privacy. I would hate if someone were listening in on me. If anyone were on the other end of my call, they would hear me beg for forgiveness. Pride was hard to swallow, but I would do it over and over again if it meant that Darren would still accept me.

I pulled the dial-back number by number while I held my breath. Darren could blow me off, and I wouldn't blame him. When I finished all the numbers, I had the phone in my hand and twirled the cord around my fingers, restless for him to pick up. The phone rang four times before I heard someone on the other end. Ring. Ring. Ring. Ring. "Hello..." I said, unsure of how to start the conversation.

Fast, jittery breathing went in and out before a little girl's voice replied, "Hi!!" Kids were conversing in the background.

"This is Penny. Who am I talking to? Is Darren there?" I said, attempting to talk over Darren's sibling's loud noise level.

"Oh! Hi, Penny. We miss you. This is Doreen! Did you watch the fireworks last night? They were so cool." Doreen was innocent and cute. I missed her simplicity.

"Yeah, I watched them for a while." I talked to Doreen about their Fourth of July and how they didn't get to use sparklers. They walked downtown by the local bar and watched the show the town put on every year. Due to its lack of funding, the show was short and uneventful. Darren's siblings had to stay close to Susan's side because she was worried about the drunken people around them. It wasn't wise to have the event so close to the tavern. Moose Creek did things to please out-of-towners, not locals with children. They had to make money somehow. I wished I could have been there to entertain them. She told me how Darren was being quiet and that their dad said he shouldn't talk to me. "How was your Fourth of July, though, Penny?"

"Oh, it was okay. Fawn got scared of all the loud explosions. I bought a pack of sparklers, which I wish I could have shared with you. I know your dad said he shouldn't talk to me, but is there any way you could put Darren on the phone?" I beseeched.

"Uh… Yeah… *Darren, phone*!" Doreen wailed.

"Hello. Who is this?" Darren's deep voice asked.

"I'm sorry. I shouldn't have pushed you away. You were right, and I miss you," I professed.

"It's okay, Copper," he said with a smile. I knew he was smiling because his voice trailed up when he did.

The conversation was going better than I thought. I could have continued asking him for forgiveness, but I knew he would tell me it was okay and to stop apologizing. As an alternative, I decided to tell him about "Pitiful Peaches."

"It's not okay. It wasn't right... Have you heard it? Your song is on the radio. Jesse Young and the Matches recorded it."

"What are you talking about? They recorded it? I haven't heard. Ever since the night we stayed out with the band, my dad has put me on lockdown. I can't go anywhere, listen to any music, and have to help him with church services. I couldn't even go watch the fireworks. Did they really record it? That's amazing! My song is on the radio!"

I fell onto my bed and swung my legs into the air as I talked. "Although the song was more than incredible, it's wrong. They didn't even mention you. You deserve some sort of recognition."

"I'm sure they mentioned me somehow. Crap. I have to go. My dad and mom are back from the store. You can't call here again. I promise I will figure out some way to talk to you. Don't worry, I forgive you. Bye!" Darren spoke in a rushed manner.

I wanted to talk to him for hours. He didn't even know about my job or daily life. I always kept Darren a close distance away because I thought if he didn't want to see or talk to me anymore it wouldn't hurt as bad. I wanted to tell him how much I messed up, and how I wanted to curl up into his arms. Or about how when I couldn't sleep at night and woke up drenched in sweat from nightmares about the night James died, I would picture Darren's face and count all the moles I could remember until I would be calm enough to go back into my dreams.

I hung up the phone and dialed a different number

that time because I couldn't let Jesse rip Darren off. Darren was the most forgiving and caring person I knew. I had to do something. I pulled the paper Mason gave me at the funeral out of my desk drawer and furiously dialed the scrawled-down integers.

Ring. Ring. Ring. Ring. Ring. Ring. Ring… Nothing.

"The number you have dialed is not available currently. If you want to leave a message, repeat it after the tone." This simple message was followed by a loud beep.

"Tonya, Mason, Keith, or whoever this is, this is Penny. I am calling because I heard the song on the radio yesterday, and I think it is great, but you know that Darren deserves some credit. Can you talk to Jesse about adding Darren's name to the song? Or at least saying that he helped write it? Please get back to me ASAP. If you need to contact Darren, you can call him yourself; I'm unable to reach him right now."

I called The Matches' number daily. My fingers memorized the calling pattern, and eventually, it became muscle memory. That number was burned into my head like a cow branding. I left over twenty messages, each one getting more resentful. I refused to give up for Darren's sake.

## Chapter Twenty-Six
## What is Right, Write

*Song: Barracuda—Heart*
*July 14th, 1975*

I was growing tired of waiting to hear from Darren or the band. And my customer service skills needed to improve. I needed to act before accidentally releasing my anger on an innocent customer at Grocery Outlet for wanting to use an expired coupon when they were penny-pinching like I do. Collecting coupons and controlling how much you spend gives you control over your life, but when you are on the other end and can't accept the coupon, it's easy to lose sight of its purpose.

My momma was doing a little better because she started cutting hair more regularly. Cutting hair made her happy and made the bills less overwhelming. I was proud of her for choosing to get out of bed each morning for something. I knew how difficult it was to put one foot in front of the other when you felt like brushing your teeth was impossible.

One day after work, I grabbed my favorite blue pen, a piece of paper from the desk set James had bought me, and sat down in my chair. I placed my new Elvis 8-track, which Betsy got me for my birthday, into the machine and began to write. My anger was rising to a head like a pimple that needed to pop to release all of its disgusting pus. Writing was the most efficient way for me to get my thoughts concise. My pen swooshed across the page, forming a music critic piece I never expected to create. I liked writing fun pieces about new albums, songs, or drama surrounding a band. One day, I planned to use my binder of writing to apply for jobs at music magazines when I got out of high school. I knew I wouldn't become the next Lester Bangs, but I could be Penny Hartley. When I finished, I pulled the page up to my lamp and read over what I wrote.

*To whom it may concern,*

*Jesse Young and The Matches is an outstanding band with many top hits and put-together albums. Still, their new single, "Pitiful Peaches," has a rather disturbing origin that correlates with theft, drug addiction, and solo careers.*

*I would like to stay anonymous for my own well-being. I have spent personal and close time with Jesse Young and the Matches and hope to alert the public about the crimes they have committed.*

*First and foremost, "Pitiful Peaches" was a short ditty that Darren Lawerence created using sheet music he found at the Moose Creek Library. He wrote the chorus and showed it to Jesse Young in confidence. He did not give the rights to the song to him, but Jesse took the initiative and added his lyrics and band to the song. Afterward, the band failed to give Darren, a high school student and aspiring music teacher, any credit or financial royalties.*

*If theft wasn't bad enough, Jesse Young has been proven to have addiction and anger management issues. He has endangered children and his bandmates by throwing glass bottles at them, verbally abusing them, and threatening them.*

*Jesse Young has been allegedly telling his bandmates that he wants to leave the band for a solo career because he is better and more talented than his co-workers. Despite his cooperation and collaboration with The Matches on the track "Pitiful Peaches," he still has proven to be a rockstar who likes throwing tantrums when things do not go his way.*

*As you can see, Jesse Young and The Matches*

*have fallen from stardom and have resorted to incredible lows to release their new top single. If you believe in the unworthy getting what they deserve, I think you will do something about it.*

*Sincerely,*

*Someone who wants the truth.*

My letter was raw, unfiltered yet professional, and perfectly conveyed my feelings. Jesse Young and The Matches had been my favorite band since James and I found their record. Sending a letter like that to magazines would put a nail in the coffin of our relationship.

Who was to say what was right and wrong? Jesse told everyone in Moose Creek that James took his own life and stole Darren's song, so maybe he deserved backlash. I pulled a clean envelope from the bottom drawer of my desk, folded the paper to fit inside, and licked it shut. Then I wrote on the cover, "Harold Hayes, Zipper Magazine Inc, 1387 N. Kirby St. Butterfield, ID, 82389." I left the return address blank.

Zipper Magazine was a newer journal that wrote columns about famous musicians, music reviews, and information about local concerts. Every now and then, when an issue came out about something I was interested in, I would buy a copy. My friends from school and I liked to get them to cut out pictures of attractive singers to keep. When I was finished analyzing the columns and choosing the photos I wanted, I would pass the magazine to my friends so they could plaster their favorites on their blank walls like a collage. I doubt they knew who their idols were under their facade.

The letter was complete and addressed to the magazine's main writer. I wasn't planning on sending it. Sending it would add another layer to it. When I returned from work, I would politely shove it into my binder and forget about its existence until I wanted to reflect on my writing. I tore down the posters of Jesse Young and The Matches from above my bed, using my bare nails to tear the paper into tiny shreds. There wasn't a need for that type of memorabilia to be in my room. Idolizing people you didn't know was stupid in the first place. I took down all my records on display and put them in a pile at the top of my closet to tuck away the past. It was time for me to go to work. I left the letter on my desk and hurried to James's truck because it was also payday. I was impatient in getting my check to finish paying last month's rent. My momma arranged a payment plan with our landlord, and I had to follow through with our word.

****

When I got home from work, I was worn out and dehydrated. My earlier rage had melted like the ice cube in the glass of water I drank. I slurped down the water and yelled at my momma that I was home. I moseyed down our hallway to my room to get changed out of my work clothes when I noticed that the letter on my desk had disappeared. I looked under my desk, on the chair, behind the desk, and on the floor. I still came up with nothing. A letter could not grow legs and walk away. It had to be in the house somewhere.

"Hey, Momma. Have you seen an envelope? It was sitting on my desk before I left!" I hollered.

My momma stuck her head into the doorframe of my room, swinging blonde strings of hair through the door, and tenderly said, "Yeah, I saw it. I put a stamp on it for you and mailed it today. I figured it would save you time, so you wouldn't have to mail it tomorrow!"

Something in my gut wrenched.

My momma was merely trying to do something good. I couldn't tell her I didn't want it mailed because she was fragile. Seeing her walk around the house and fold laundry was an accomplishment, so I imposed a weak smile of appreciation and mustered out the word, "Thanks."

A day working with the public made a person understand that everyone had their quirks. I was ignorant to think that celebrities and rock stars weren't perfect. The entire world would see Jesse Young and The Matches in a different light as a consequence of my writing and my momma's obnoxious kindness.

I couldn't tell if our mailbox's flag was raised or not. I wondered if I could save it. I dashed out the front door, through our yard, and arrived at our mailbox out of breath. I put my hands on my knees before I opened the flap. My knees were spotless and smooth. The previous scars faded over the weeks I was home. I flipped the flap open to see the metal box was vacant, and the red flag was down. It was too late. I anticipated the worst outcome as I sat alone on the road's curb, letting the loose gravel fall through my fingertips.

## Chapter Twenty-Seven
## On the Rise

*Song: You're So Vain—Carly Simon*
*July 17th, 1975*

I started to forget about the existence of my harmful letter arriving at Zipper Magazine headquarters. I thought that by then someone would have read the letter to decide if it was good enough to release it to the press. Zipper's silence led me to believe there was nothing to worry about. My writing didn't captivate Harold Hayes enough, which deflated my confidence in my writing skills, but it was good for my relationship with Jesse Young and the Matches if I ever wanted to reunite our friendship.

Darren contacted Betsy, who called me to say, "Darren misses you and is trying his best to leave the teeny town of Moose Creek to be with you." She blabbed on and on about all the little things Thomas was failing at doing as her boyfriend. "He's just not very romantic anymore. I don't know what to do about it. It might be best if we just go back to being friends. I need a man who will give me butterflies whenever I see them."

At first, I was uneasy about what their complicated relationship would do to our friend group, but I was one to talk. I had changed every dynamic in our group, and I wasn't convinced I could go back to Moose Creek. So why did it matter? Betsy was wrong, though. Relationships weren't about big romantic gestures. They were about the tiny things that added up and the loyalty of choosing to stay with someone despite every outside factor.

Talking to Betsy made me miss Moose Creek. Darren hated living at a boring pinpoint on a map with his demanding father and religious upbringing. Moose Creek meant more to me than that because it was my family's getaway. Without James, we had no place to visit even if we wanted to. The town did not have a hotel we could rent, and we needed a camper if we wanted to park anywhere we wished. I would miss the cold streams to swim in, the peach merchandise, the townspeople, the days spent playing basketball or hanging out in the park, and the privilege of running around without any threat to my safety. Butterfield was an all right city, with a population exceeding fifty thousand. We had movie theaters, places to hold concerts, multiple city parks, and any restaurant we needed. The bigger population made it less safe and cozy, though. When I desired something new yet familiar, Moose Creek was there for me to fall back on, but it was ripped away from me. I had nowhere to run when life got tedious.

Boy, was life tedious. The only people I interacted with were my momma and co-workers. I was supposed to be having the best summer of my life, but James's decision to end his life had altered my plan for the future. My emotions were confused. I could go from being vexed at James to devastated, missing him, upset, and then feeling guilty. The process of grieving was complex and was something I was grateful to do on my own terms, even if I was lonely. I understood my grandma in ways I never imagined. The way she would snap and demand attention was wrong, and yet I felt like snapping all the time after James died.

I often checked the magazine inventory at work to see the newest additions of Zipper Magazine. Our work policy said customers could only open a magazine if they bought it because too many people would read the content and put it back on the shelf without paying a dime, so I began buying each monthly copy. I noticed a new edition of Zipper, even though there was already one out for the month of July.

The front cover pictured two ginormous peaches lying in the grass against each other, with a bite taken out of the closest peach showing a glimpse of its brown pit. The title read, "ZIPPER: PITIFUL PEACHES or STOLEN SECRETS?" In fine print, it said, "Look on page eight to find out!" I almost ripped the magazine open when my boss walked by. I pretended to put the magazine back into the slot despite wanting more than anything to read what was inside that cover.

"Hey! I am facing the new stock of magazines," I said slyly. Facing is when you bring products toward the front of a shelf so customers can reach them more easily.

Fernando gave me a thumbs-up as he observed me.

Employees could only buy personal items during their breaks or when off the clock. My break was an hour away, and I wondered if I would survive until then. The minutes seemed to pass as slowly as Sheriff Douglas could run. It was agonizing seeing the clock tick forward with such little movement. When it was finally time to get my fingers onto the publication, I bolted down the aisle, grabbed the peach cover, and placed it on the conveyor belt. The magazine pushed forward as my co-worker Marvin rang it up for me.

"Are you a fan of Jesse Young and the Matches? I think that new song stinks. Disco is where the trends are heading. You should come to the roller rink to get your groove on. Sometimes, some other workers and I go there after work. They play the best songs. It feels great under the sparkling lights. I'd love to take you."

I wouldn't be caught dead roller skating, especially listening to disco in some sequin outfit. It wasn't my scene, and neither was Marvin. Marvin was an all right guy and was only a grade above me but was part of an incompatible social group. Not to mention, my heart was elsewhere.

"Oh, thanks for the offer, but I don't think it would be for me. I am more of a rock fan," I said, grabbing the magazine and rushing out the front door. "I will be back! I am taking my break!" Although I listened to other genres occasionally, I needed an excuse to get out of there.

I sat in the front seat and felt the pages between my fingertips, licking my thumb to turn them. After picking apart a couple of pages that were stuck together, I flipped to page eight, revealing more than the story I wrote in my letter.

*PITIFUL PEACHES or STOLEN SECRETS?*

By: Harrold Hayes

*If you haven't heard Jesse Young and The Matches' new hit "Pitiful Peaches," you are in for a treat. The song has something for everybody to love; relatable lyrics, soft piano, electric bass, and a moody drum beat. But is it original?*

*An anonymous source wrote to ZIPPER claiming that Pitiful Peaches' lyrics were stolen from a high school student named Darren Lawrence in Moose Creek, and the sequence of chords on the chorus were made by a 1950s band called Brett Beats. Lawyers from Brett Beats are thoroughly looking into the situation and claiming they will also represent Mr. Lawrence if they file a lawsuit against the band and Ultimate Records.*

*Jesse Young's fame may be going to his head, making fans worried for his health and well-being. After a concert disaster in Portland, Oregon, Jesse went AWOL. Concertgoers say that Jesse was upset at his bandmate, Keith Knox, for changing the setlist. Jesse allegedly threw his microphone at Keith, causing the mic to make a high-pitched noise. Many fans are outraged and are demanding a refund. Jesse Young and The Matches have refused to respond to any of these newfound allegations.*

*A guilty photo has emerged of Jesse Young at West-Brooke Rehabilitation Center, where he has been admitted. The public is left to ask if "Pitiful Peaches" is a masterpiece or "Stolen Secrets."*

Next to the column was a blurry black-and-white paparazzi photograph of Jesse smoking a cigarette on a balcony. He wore jeans with a plain white cotton shirt that was baggy compared to his typical well-fitted show attire. His tattooed arms looked weak in the overflow of the cloth. It could have been the low quality or the shadows from the sun, but the corner of his mouth was raised like he was about to smile. A wave of guilt hit me, pushed me over, and dragged me in the current.

CHAYLEE McCLEESE

## Chapter Twenty-Eight
## Spit Out the Pit

*Song: Vienna—Billy Joel*
*July 20th, 1975*

I told myself the article could be worse. It barely included what I wrote. Yes, it mentioned stealing the song, but Darren deserved credit for his work. I didn't know who Brett's Beat was, and it was their sheet music Darren took, so they should have been credited as well. My letter couldn't have been the first one they received about Jesse. The concert in Portland sounded worse than what I said. Jesse's pain was valid, along with their fans' outrage. If I went to a concert that ended in a brawl, I would want a refund, too.

The new edition was flying off Grocery Outlet's shelves, and it made me want to go back and put my name on the letter because Zipper had to be making a ton of money off the story. I wasn't greedy, but I couldn't work as many hours when summer ended, and money would be tight.

People in Butterfield worshiped the ground Jesse Young and The Matches walked on. It wasn't every day that a famous band could come from our area. The article put a wrench in everyone's beliefs, including my own. I knew that Jesse had issues and seeing him standing on the balcony made me feel a little spark of hope. He was getting some sort of help. He asked for help when needed, which was more than most people. However, if Jesse had read the article, he would know I wrote to Zipper, and I doubt he would be so forgiving of me.

When I got home, my momma asked how my day was, and I pined for someone to talk to about the article. Her hair was cut even shorter than before. She must have found her clippers and went to work while I was gone. Hundreds of hair clippings were lying in the bathroom trash. Her hair was nearly the same length as Tonya's. The short strands framed her face, making her chin more prominent and sharper. I handed her the magazine, expecting a harsh reaction. When she reached the end of the page, she laughed hysterically.

"Oh my God. You sent them a letter. Was this what it was about? My Penny is feuding with rock n' roll stars already. What am I going to do with you?" she said sarcastically.

"I wasn't going to send the letter. Before I could interject, you stamped it and threw it in the mailbox. I don't know if I did the right thing, Momma," I said, laying everything out in the open.

"Nothing is black and white. If you felt it was wrong, then it was. If you feel guilty and think it's bad, then you learned your lesson," she advised me. I wanted her to yell at me like a normal parent would for once. I wanted to feel something. Momma wasn't the type of parent to yell, though, and she wasn't in any shape to raise her voice.

"He's at that rehabilitation center. I wish James would have at least said he was hurting. Jesse can be awful, but he is trying. I'm scared I hurt him even more with that letter. I seem to be hurting many people recently," I acknowledged.

"Then make it up to him. I need to make it up to you, Sweetie. I haven't been a very responsible mother. You shouldn't have to be supporting our family. I am going to look for a job. It's only right. After James died, I didn't want to face reality. I am still alive because of you. You are my baby, and you still need me, even if you have grown up so much and are starting to like boys and are becoming a writer." She nudged me.

"Boys? I didn't even tell you about Darren, did I? How did you know? It's okay, Momma. I like working at the grocery store. It keeps my mind off things, and I feel good helping you. I know things have been rough. I miss him so much. Your hair looks nice. I like the new look. It makes you look tough," I said, touching her new doo. She did look adamant, like a person who could handle her own business without a man dictating what she could or couldn't do.

My momma drew me in close to her chest and clenched my shoulders. Things had been out of order since James died, and the woman holding me had changed. She was more assertive, responsible, and had a different haircut, but she was still my mother. She instinctively knew what was happening inside my head and how to ease my sorrows. Now that we were on the same page, I felt less alone.

"I would make it up to Jesse and the Matches if they would answer their phone. I tried calling them multiple times. It is what it is, I guess. I definitely won't make the same mistake again. I learned my lesson: don't write when you are angry, especially to popular magazines. How are you doing, Momma? I know how I feel. I couldn't imagine how you feel. He was your soulmate."

"It was so sudden. I didn't think I would lose James until I grew old and gray," Momma admitted.

"I knew he got sad sometimes and wanted a different job. I had no idea he was that bad."

"I knew, Sweetie. There is only so much you can do. He wanted to look strong to you. He didn't want you to see how badly he was struggling. He saw how much you looked toward him as a role model and didn't want to mess that up. I tried to get him to see a doctor. He didn't want to go."

"I wished he would have told me. Everyone is messed up. He wasn't alone in his feelings. I didn't even ask you where you were when he died because I didn't want to upset you. As you know, I was with Jesse Young and The Matches. I should have gone home earlier or somehow called him. Maybe if I did…"

"It wouldn't have made a difference. I went to my friend's house to discuss some new Avon products. James said he would be fine and was going to watch some TV. I got caught up in girl talk, drank some wine, and lost track of time. When I heard the sirens, I thought of him, and you know the rest," Momma explained.

"It's okay, Momma. We both got lost."

"We are more alike than you think. You are my girl. We will figure this out. We need time to heal," my momma said, bringing me a sliver of relief.

## Chapter Twenty-Nine
## Make Amends

*Song: Three Steps to Heaven—Showaddywaddy*
*July 18th, 1975*

It was my day off work, and the morning energy crept through my window blinds, forcing me to get out of bed. I rubbed my eyelids and stretched my legs, pointing my toes toward the light. On my days off, I liked to play with Fawn, clean the house for my momma, and read when I got the chance. I stayed busy to keep my mind from drifting too far away.

I went to the kitchen to pour myself a cup of coffee, a habit I picked up from having to get up early to unload the trucks at work. I sat at the dining table, sipping the caffeine and appreciating the flowers outside the window. A yellow bird sat on James's hood, tweeting a simple tune. The bird reminded me of James when he used to tap his foot even when music was absent. James had music running through his bloodstream, and he would get it out any way he could.

I needed to go to the school district office to pick my sophomore year classes and schedule. I wasn't ready to return to school because it meant explaining what had happened to my classmates and teachers. It also meant less time working, less money, and time away from Darren. I hoped that Darren wouldn't be upset that I'd written to Zipper. I wished I could talk to him and hear his deep voice telling me everything would be okay.

I cared less about my looks than I did before. I had no one to impress except myself. My wardrobe consisted of employee shirts and James's band Ts. I threw on his white Who shirt and told my momma it was time to go. My mom had to tag along to sign some paperwork for the school. Before we left, I picked some flowers in front of the kitchen window and put them on the truck's dash. They were going out of season and would wither away. Plus, I was excited to freshen the musky smelling truck up with the scent of petals.

When we arrived at the office, I knotted the shirt up so it wouldn't look like I wasn't wearing shorts. I was simply going through the motions. I rang the silver bell on the counter, and a secretary with gray hair pulled up in a tight, neat bun greeted us.

"Good morning! You must be Penelope and Penelope's mother! It's great to see you guys. Penelope, you can head into Mr. Carrey's office to pick up your classes while your mother stays here and fills out paperwork."

I hesitantly went into Mr. Carrey's office. Mr. Carrey was the school district's counselor. He had a kind, gentle face, bright white teeth, and short brown hair. He was on the younger side of being a counselor, yet he was terrific at his job.

"Hello, Penelope. Take a seat. In front of you are classes for you to choose from. Go ahead and give it a look! When I glanced at your records, I noticed how well you performed in your Language Arts class, and I suggest you take a couple of Honors classes this year."

I moved the pen to mark all the classes I wanted to take. There were many different classes, but some stood out to me more. I circled Honor's ELA, Algebra 2, U.S. History, Biology, Music Appreciation, and Intro to Journalism. I slid the paper back toward him.

Mr. Carrey nodded, approving my choices. "Perfect, this would be a great fit for you. I believe that we can make this work."

"Thanks, what is Music Appreciation like?"

"Oh, it's a fun class! You learn about music's

history, how to play an instrument, and study famous artists like the band on your shirt!"

"Okay, cool. Thanks, Mr. Carrey," I said, rising from the uncomfortable chair to leave.

"If you need anything else, don't hesitate to reach out! My door is always open for students in need," he said, using his eyes to tell me he knew about James. Everyone in Moose Creek knew James was dead. I didn't know how long would it take for word to spread around Butterfield.

"Um, yeah, thanks. See you," I said.

"Just so you know, it's normal to feel numb after a traumatic experience. Your brain is a wonderful tool. When it experiences something that it cannot handle, it sometimes blocks the memory altogether. Your body ends up being in this limbo state where you don't feel like yourself. Journaling or writing is a great tool to get it all out," he informed me.

"Interesting. Thanks," I said, closing his door behind me.

My momma was still filling out paperwork.

The secretary pointed to a line on the paper in front of her, stating, "Sign here."

Standing behind my mom, I realized why we were there in the first place. Registration was typically in the second week of August, but we registered in July. I thought it was because sophomores had more seniority than first-year students. That wasn't the case. We were there for my mom to change the paperwork of my emergency contacts and guardianship because James was no longer with us. It was also a chance for my mom to make me see a counselor to make sure I was okay. I wished she would see a counselor instead.

I was happy about my new classes because they reflected my interests, so I decided not to make a fuss about the appointment. I was fine. I wasn't perfect, but grief wasn't ideal, and although Mr. Carrey was a safe person to talk to, I didn't have anything new to get out. Time was the only thing that could help me. I was starting to come out of the limbo he was talking about, and it was more painful than when it first happened.

My mother took the keys from me to drive home. "I want to drive back," she told me. She started to take an alternate route. I pondered where she was taking me. We went past the corner store in the opposite direction of my work and turned on an unfamiliar road. The cemetery came into view. It had bright green grass, a cement building in the middle, and narrow walkways throughout the court. Some graves were decorated with flowers, American flags, and garlands; others were plain and bare. The plain plots blended into the grass, making the dead seem forgotten.

"Why are we here?" I asked my mother, scared of what was to come.

"Let's go see James."

I grabbed the flowers on the dash so I wouldn't be visiting him empty-handed and followed my mom between the labyrinth of headstones.

After wandering around, zigzagging through the rows, my mom came to a complete stop. The headstone was marble and smaller than the others in size. Under his name, "James Hartley," an eighth note was engraved. On the left side of the words was an oval-shaped picture of James. His mustache was styled up, and his lips pursed together, forming a no-teeth smile. It was a colored photo of him from the day he took me to my first concert. Colored photos were expensive. Seeing his face was nice, as I used to see him every day. I kneeled on the grass, putting the flowers I picked in the morning over his stone. I had seen some people treat grave sites as visiting places to talk to the dead. Talking to a stone was more awkward to me than comforting. Momma leaned down to kiss his picture and rub the stone goodbye. She then led me back to the pickup, gripping my shoulders as we walked by various freshly dug plots.

As I snapped my seatbelt closed, my momma said, "I have a surprise for you, Sweetie. I know I need a real job, and hair is my passion. I am going to beauty school! My friend Heather has a salon, and they will teach me everything from hair dye to nails. When I pass the course, they will hire me full-time."

"That's great news, Mom. How are you going to pay for the class, though?"

"I have my way," she deviously said.

She had to have been up to something. Despite visiting James's grave for the first time, she returned to her usual peppy and inspirational self. Money didn't grow on trees, which made her careless attitude concerning. I did not know how she paid for the headstone either.

"I am happy for you, Momma, but we should discuss this. I could pick up a couple of extra shifts to get the money for the class. I don't want us to struggle more than we already are. I think that this is a good thing. We must be responsible about it, though," I said, trying to crunch numbers in my head.

"Sweetie, I said I have it covered."

I wasn't paying attention to the teal VW bus in the driveway, or the people huddled around our door. I was so focused on trying to help my mom accomplish her dream, thinking about school and James's grave, that it took me a minute to put two and two together.

Darren, Jesse Young, and The Matches sat on our porch stoop, waiting for us to get home. The band was styled back in their usual attire. Darren smiled when he saw us whipping into the driveway, and I couldn't help but smile back. Smiling could be contagious if you let it be. The entire band's eyes creased, and lips rose while I stared at them.

"Did you plan this?" I questioned my mom.

She shrugged and said, "I told you I had to make it up to you. What are you waiting for?"

## Chapter Thirty
## Resilience

*Song: Wish You Were Here—Pink Floyd*
*July 18th, 1975*

Darren hugged and squeezed me tightly. I was a ripe peach, finally ready to be picked. The Matches gave me genuine hugs in addition to Darren's embrace. When I got to Jesse, his eyes lit up, and he said, "Good to see you, Penny! We have much to discuss."

Jesse's face was not as rigid, and something about his aurora had changed.

We had more than "much" to talk about. I last spoke to Jesse and the band at the funeral. My world had changed dramatically since that day in the church, and I didn't know where to start. I encouraged them to come inside to be a good host, and they hurried in to sit in our quaint living space.

Keith complimented our bright yellow circle pillows as he got situated on the couch. My momma kept our house spotless and decorated with flare. She liked things to match and put thought into each piece in each room.

"I am sorry for writing to Zipper," I blurted out.

"Don't worry about it. That magazine has been following us around everywhere. They saw the Portland show and were bound to write a piece anyway—water under the bridge. We messed up, too. I should have given Darren credit. The label didn't want to add more names to the roster. I could have tried more," Jesse claimed.

"Yeah, but it was wrong. I was angry at everything and took it out on you. I should have tried to talk to you all about it. I tried to call that number Tonya and Mason gave me."

Fawn greeted Mason by jumping onto his lap and licking his face.

"That would be my fault. I gave you the wrong number. We had to get a new number when our old number leaked. Fans try to find our number like FBI detectives, so we change it here and there. I am sorry, Penny. We girls need to stick together. I will get you Ronny's number. That way, we can stay in touch," Tonya said, while scratching her head.

"Oh," I said, wondering about who got all the nasty voicemails I left.

"Ronny showed us the article, and we went into pursuit of finding you and Darren. We had to make it up to you two kids," Mason said as rubbing Fawn's ear.

"I appreciate it. I only want Darren to get credit, so we are on good terms if you do that."

"They are going to do more than that, Copper," Darren said, raising his voice an octave up.

My momma placed her hands in her lap, trying to contain herself. What was going on? It seemed like everyone was in cahoots except me.

"We have been in contact with your mom and Darren for a while and have decided to help your family. I am so sorry for how I behaved around you and your friends. I was hurting and didn't know how to reach out. When I saw what losing James did to your family, I knew I needed to change. The day after the funeral, I got clean and recorded the song. My agents sent it out way too early. I'm not perfect, but I am trying," Jesse stated.

"That explains the picture at the Westbrooke Rehabilitation Center. So, what have all of you been discussing without me?" I demanded to know. Westbrooke had many different floors. Some helped people detox when they were addicted to something, others were for people who were depressed, and the top floor was for people who couldn't live on their own. Jesse was either on the first or second floor. The picture was on a balcony, so I figured he ended up being on the second.

"Well, we have decided to hold a concert benefit in honor of James. All of the profits will go toward your family. Your mom can attend beauty school, and you won't always have to work. You can focus on school. Your mom told us you are a good student; we wouldn't want anything to interrupt that. We will also start some sort of fund so you can go to college if you want to," Mason revealed.

"Are you pulling my leg? This cannot be real. James would be ecstatic if you are playing in Butterfield again. He wanted to take me to one of your live shows."

Jesse stood up, placing his thumbs into his pockets and moving his body back and forth. "That is exactly why it will pull in more money than you could dream. Your mother also found some sponsors for the event." Who would sponsor an event for a dead guy they didn't know very well? Who cared enough to help us out?

Jesse unfolded a green flyer from his pocket and gave it to me. It was my favorite shade of green. Darren must have helped design the handout and suggested making it that color. The flyer said, "Grocery Outlet and The Peach Pot present Jesse Young and The Matches Benefit Concert in honor of James Hartley." The front of the brochure was fun, energetic, and lively. There was a graphic of a stage, a microphone, and the same picture of James on his headstone. That picture had to be my momma's doing. At the very bottom of the flyer in fine print, it read, "Special Guests: Darren Lawerence and Bret Beats!" Benefits were typically slow and dull. The concert would bring people together without crying or having long, dreadful conversations. James would have chosen to go to a concert over a funeral any day.

I wanted to run and tell James that things could get better. I imagined dancing around the living room with him and introducing him to the amiable people surrounding me. People did care. I allowed my raw emotions to come out, making droplets of joy fall onto James's white shirt.

"Thank you so much," I said.

****

"Do you want to stay for dinner? I bet you all are starving after driving all the way out here," Momma asked.

"I could eat. Recently, I got a real sweet tooth," Jesse said, seemingly replacing one addiction with another.

"Sounds like someone I know," I said, nudging Darren.

"All right, sit tight! Penny, why don't you take the band out onto the carport or the backyard? Give them a tour of the house. It is the least we can do for them."

It was peculiar showing my favorite band around our house. It wasn't anything spectacular like what they were probably used to. As I gestured toward my bedroom, I was glad I tore down my posters of them. I would have looked like a crazy fangirl if they were still plastered to the wall. Stuffed animals lay on my bed, revealing my inner girlhood. It was also the first time Darren saw where I lived. I closed my door, hoping he wouldn't comment on the giant giraffe stuffed animal I had or my floral bedspread. We walked down our narrow hallway as I pointed out each room and showed them where the bathroom was in case they needed to use it. I was used to my voice echoing throughout the house, but it was stuffy with all our bodies crammed inside.

"Why don't we head outside? It's a little cramped

in here," I suggested.

I led the band to our backyard.

My momma was already wiping off our outdoor table and chairs with a rag so the band could sit. Fawn ran around the yard while Darren helped me puff our umbrella over the table. Momma made everyone sit down as she returned to the kitchen and got to work. She was overjoyed to be cooking for someone again. She didn't like cooking for only two people because we always had leftovers. She brought out a small platter of snacks to fill our bellies while we waited.

"So, this is where you grew up? You see my house every summer. It's ridiculous. This is my first time seeing where you come from," Darren commented.

"Yeah, sorry. It's not much."

"Not much? This house is so peaceful and charming," Tonya said.

"I wish I grew up in a nice house like this," Keith added.

"You know what? It is more than nice. I don't know why I'm acting like it isn't. James put his soul into this house for us. He mowed the lawn, raked the leaves in the fall, helped repair anything that needed to be repaired, and still wanted more for us." It was difficult to talk about James, but it was something I needed to start doing. Writing about him was easier.

"More isn't what it's cracked up to be, as you have learned," Jesse said, pulling his boots off the table as Momma brought us our dinner plates.

"I agree to that. You are starting to sound like me, Jesse," Mason said.

Momma brought out a gigantic bowl of salad, warm buns, mashed potatoes, vegetables, and some chicken. She balanced the plates and bowls between her arms as she set them down. "Dinner is served."

The band dug into the food like starving animals, pulling apart the chicken with their teeth like they hadn't had a fresh meal in years. After eating a bite, they would murmur how good it was and how thankful they were for it.

"Oh, you are too generous. It's just something I whipped together," my momma gushed.

Mason looked starstruck. He barely talked as he thoroughly tested his food. By the time everyone had finished their plates, their guts were bloated, and everyone became sleepy.

"Mrs. Hartley, I have to know your recipes. That dinner was spectacular," Mason said to Momma. The two of them went into our house. When they returned, Mason carried a tray of homemade muffins and a piece of paper with some of Momma's best recipes. They looked like two friends having a normal conversation.

"Are those muffins? Thanks, April. I will eat these later," Jesse said, taking the plate away from Mason's grasp.

They called it a night once the band could stand up without having their jeans rip open. Jesse rented a motel room for Darren and the rest of the band.

"We should leave for the night. We appreciated the dinner, Mrs. Hartley," Tonya said.

"Yeah, thanks. It's been a while since I've had a real meal. I do love road food, though," Keith admitted.

My momma gave them proper goodbyes as they piled into the bus. We waved at them until we couldn't see the glow of their taillights anymore.

## Chapter Thirty-One
## My First Concert

*Song: Love Reign O'er Me—The Who*
*November 5th, 1973*

***Penny: Don't worry, Harold. I'm going to tell you about this memory too. I got the hang of this now.***

***Harold Hayes: Yes, you do.***

On November 5th, 1973, James took me to my first concert to celebrate becoming my official guardian. When my dad left, I still had his last name, which confused people when my mother's and mine didn't match. She was a Hartley, and I was a Roberts. I didn't feel like I was a Roberts at all. My dad had no idea who I was or when my birthday was, and James knew every little detail about me. I was transported to heaven when he presented the idea of adopting me. My spirit was as light as a feather. He also wanted to adopt my sister, Breanna, but didn't because she chose not to. She was also almost eighteen, so adopting her wouldn't have done anything to change her life like it would mine.

We went to the courthouse to provide all the proper documentation of my mom and his marriage, as well as my birth certificate. The clerk told us the only way James could adopt me was if my dad signed away all legal rights for me. I was devastated because I thought that my dad lived thousands of miles away and was uncontactable. The clerk gave us the paper to send him anyway, and we went home.

A few days later, my momma presented me with the document. My dad's precise signature was on a dotted line at the bottom of the page. I was too afraid to ask how she got his signature so promptly. If he was living in

Butterfield, wouldn't my momma tell me? I didn't understand why he didn't want to be a part of my life. He left our family and abandoned me. However, it didn't matter because it meant James would become my father legally. James raised me and was my father before any paperwork was signed, but then it became official.

James bought us tickets to see The Who live in concert to celebrate our new legally bonding family. He wanted my first concert to be Jesse Young and The Matches, but their tours tended to skip over Butterfield. The Who recently released the double album "Quadrophenia," a rock opera following an intense and fun story. The Who was the closest concert we could attend, and they were a band we liked, so we thought it was better than nothing. Listening to the opera on vinyl was one thing, but hearing it in person was transformative.

The concert house was the most enormous room I had ever entered. Hundreds of fans were already pushed against the front of the stage, expecting Roger Daltrey's curly blond hair and Keith Moon's sweat-drenched face as he raised his drumsticks.

Women wore skimpy clothing, and men dressed like the band. James was dressed in his usual attire: cowboy boots, a flannel button-up long-sleeve shirt, and baggy jeans. My momma wanted to stay home with my sister, so only James and I attended the concert. My momma and sister helped me pick a new shirt the previous week. It had strange cutouts on the front and was short-sleeved.

James stood tall, towering over me, grabbing my hand, and guiding me through the crowd. Feet and trash covered the floor. The crowded nature of concerts intimidated me, but I was there for the music, so I stood my ground. Bodies pushed past me, trying to get closer and closer to the action, making me raise my shoulders to look more developed and robust than I was.

James shoved us into the middle section of the pit. He held my arm and told me not to let go because he didn't want to be separated during the show. The room was so loud I couldn't hear myself think. People were talking, dancing, drinking, smoking, and kissing. The lights dimmed, and I stood on my tippy toes, trying to see over the tall man before me. There should be some sort of concert etiquette where tall people stayed toward the back. People were selfish and wanted to have the best view. James pulled me in and had me get on his shoulders. I looked around, seeing the tops of people's heads instead of the back of their calves. Large spotlights were faced toward separate parts of the stage. Anticipation filled the room.

Roger Daltrey came onto the stage wearing flared jeans and an open shirt. His chest aimed toward his screaming fans, inviting them to look at his body for the rest of the night. The remaining band members came onto the stage, and James yelled at me, "You can scream too!"

I restrained. Screaming at the top of my lungs was strange and untraditional, so I opened my mouth and squeaked. It was not a full-blown scream, but it was a start. My screams got louder, deeper, and more pronounced throughout the concert. James rooted me on and yelled with me. Our voices blended in with the others in the room. I could yell the lyrics, and no one would hear my individual voice because everyone else was singing along, too.

The walls vibrated and shook to the rhythm. I could feel the beat in every inch of my body. Lights flashed, fog smeared over us, and James was shoved. Nasty-smelling beer spilled on him, yet he kept his legs buckled to the floor. He wanted me to have a good time, and I did. I had the best seat in the house. I was a part of a family and something bigger.

Being a fan was not just supporting a band or artists because you liked them. It was a community. It was a way of life. One girl who swept past us told us it was her fifth Who concert that month. You had to have a passion to follow something so devoutly. After that concert, I knew I wanted to be a part of the music community. It gave meaning to my life. I think James felt the same way. He couldn't shake the smile off his face, even days later.

## Chapter Thirty-Two
## Stage Fright

*Song: Let It Be—The Beatles*
*August 1st, 1975*

The day of the benefit concert finally arrived. Momma cut my hair for it. It was time for a change, so I decided on bangs like hers. Curly wisps of my blonde hair shot up, covering my forehead. I liked the way they dangled down like a show curtain. I got my peach necklace out of my jewelry box and clasped it at the front of my chest, moving the peach locket to the front. I didn't have to open the locket to know that my family and James remained inside, untouched and still alive. Momma dropped me off at the field the band rented for the event.

I looked for potential in the tall, swaying yellow grass field. Darren had alerted me that a crew would appear soon to put up a stage for the concert. Jesse Young and The Matches would rest at their motel until later, leaving Darren and me alone. I wondered how his dad reacted when he asked if he could run off with a famous rock n' roll band to see me and drum in a concert.

Darren's face displayed much more maturity than even at the beginning of the summer. He was ready for commitment and responsibilities, and so was I.

I wrapped my arms around his waist and placed my head against his chest. "How are you here? Isn't your dad fuming?"

"I sort of left. By the way, I like the new hair," Darren said, not letting me pull away from him this time.

"Thanks. You left and didn't ask him?" I questioned.

"I didn't ask him if I could come. I told him I was

coming here to see you and to help your family, and he could do nothing to stop me. He has kept me there too long and needs to realize that if he is going to treat me like an adult, I can make my own decisions."

"Wow. I am proud of you for standing up for yourself. I know how hard it can be for you. Are you scared he will punish you when you get back?"

"If he punishes me, he will lose a babysitter. He knows he doesn't have power over me anymore. It's not like I am doing anything bad. Last time I checked, love is the best reason to do something, anyway."

"About that … I was wondering if the offer still stands..."

"Yes, Copper!"

"I didn't even finish what I was going to say. How do you know?"

"You were going to say you want to be my girlfriend."

We would still need to figure out how a distance relationship would work or how often we would get to see each other, but Darren was right for me. He was more than I could ask for. In his arms, I was safe. I wasn't worried he would leave me anymore because his actions had proven otherwise. He went against his dad and didn't let life get in the way. I was still scared to commit, but it was easier when he wasn't just a boy who wanted a summer fling. He wanted something more profound than the creek's surface. He wanted someone who would dive into the freezing water without hesitation, and I was honored to jump in for him, like he did for me.

Fifty or so men in black security shirts showed up and pulled out long metal pieces from their trucks. They worked alongside each other like ants, obeying their queen to build the stage. By noon, the plain field became a vast arena for people who loved music. A long banner that stated, "In memory of James Hartley" was hung at the top of the stage.

Another group of men added microphones, drums, a keyboard, and amp hookups to the platform. I helped hang up concert flyers around town and directed crew members where to go. Everything was falling into place. Some of my Grocery Outlet co-workers volunteered to transform the field into a breathtaking event, and they did by placing decorations throughout the area.

The Peach Pot set up a large tent to sell peach ice cream and raise funds in addition to a few food trucks. Ronny made a booth to sell new Jesse Young and The Matches Pitiful Peaches shirts. The slick design was bound to sell out quickly. The ROCK 105.1's radio host set up camp in their company van across the street to narrate the event. The station's van was wrapped in a tie-dye design with big block letters of their station on the side. I couldn't believe that James would be talked about on the radio. I wanted more than anything to tell him. James's benefit concert was the biggest event of the summer. It was endearing to see everyone pulling together to put it on.

People flowed through the gates toward the stage. Excited energy buzzed through the air as more bodies piled beside each other, coming together for a common interest. James would have been obsessed with the benefit. He would have said that it proved how music had healing properties that could change someone's life. I hoped he was somewhere in the clouds, looking down on us and singing along. He wasn't a saint, but he was a good man. Deep down I knew he was in a better place.

Backstage, Bret Beats prepared to be the first act. Bret Beats turned out to be an old high school band. They did not become famous, tour, or even record any albums. They made the sheet music for "Pitiful Peaches" and went separate ways when they received their high school diplomas in Moose Creek. One member became an accountant, one passed away, and another was a school bus driver. The members of Bret Beats were pleased their work was used and perplexed about how it came to be.

Ronny reached out to the surviving members and asked for the rights to the song. They agreed to sign the copyright and perform as an opener to Jesse Young and The Matches if they got a small profit cut. The older men were delicate yet knew how to work a crowd. Their stage presence allowed for a simple and sweet start to the benefit. They played classic song covers from Elvis to Johnny Cash. Bret Beats was the sort of band you would hire for a birthday party or county fair. Audience members took their partner's hands and danced around the stage. Other peers took the extra time before the main act to buy goodies from the various vendors.

The diverse crowd included families, truckers James knew, rock n' roll fans, and locals who wanted to support the cause. One man stood out to me. He wore office clothes in the heat and carried a notepad with a pencil tucked behind his ear. The abnormal man made eye contact with me like he was trying to figure out who I was. He gradually walked toward me and introduced himself as Harold Hayes, a writer from Zipper Magazine. I shook his hand as he said, "A little birdy wrote to me. Does that bird happen to be standing in front of me? I expected you to be a boy, but obviously, you aren't."

"Maybe," I replied, oblivious to what he wanted.

"Your letter was interesting. If you have time to talk, I would love to see some of your other writing," Harold said as he fixed a crease in his slacks.

Darren, who was uneasy with his presence at first, gave me a look of approval. I thought of my binder full of random writing pieces that, although I believed in them, I only pictured them getting published as a dream.

"I think I could round up a couple of pieces of writing samples to share with you if you would like to exchange contact information," I said as formally as possible. If I were going to make it into the publishing world, I needed to sound polished, especially as a young girl.

"Sounds like a plan to me, little bird. I would like to hear your tweets about this concert as well." I wrote my phone number and address on Harold's pad and shook his hand firmly.

Darren and I went backstage to talk to the band before they switched out.

"Congratulations, Copper. You just made your first connection in the music publishing space."

He was right. I was moving up in the world. A connection could mean more chances of publishing my writing. It could mean that I could do what James wanted for me. James had spent every moment he could preparing me for a world without him, and now that he was gone, I could power through, but I still craved his guidance.

"Congratulations to you. You are about to perform at your first real concert," I praised Darren back. We found Jesse Young and The Matches huddled together on the right side of the stage behind a long red curtain. "Hey, I can't believe how many people are here. You guys outdid yourselves," I said, thanking the band.

"Ah, it's nothing compared to some of the shows we have played. Those Bret Beats are some funny old geezers. We are pumped to get out there and perform. How are you feeling, Darry? Are you ready to play in front of that crowd," Jesse snarked.

Darren nodded as he twitched his fingers. "Yeah."

"You will do great. You are going to play backup

for me. I will be right by your side," Keith said, consoling Darren's nerves.

Tonya glanced at her watch with a cheeky grin. "It's time."

The members of Bret Beats walked off stage to get dinner for their reunion with each other.

Jesse wore one of his tight button-up shirts with flared jeans. He wore his show clothes like armor.

Mason pulled me aside to talk. "The plan is to introduce ourselves and the cause, and we will call you on stage to talk briefly about James if you feel comfortable. Also, beware of Jesse. This will be his first show sober, and he won't know how to act. He just ate an entire box of snack packs."

It was wild to think that Jesse was sober. He did seem more alert and down to earth, but he didn't possess his regular pizazz. Jesse was electric when he was under the influence. I wasn't sure if anyone had seen him clean since they released their first album. Getting drunk was his pre-show ritual, so he needed something new to hype him up. Snack Packs could do the trick, but for how long? I hoped he would seek out more help.

"Harold Hayes is here, a critic from Zipper, so this needs to go well."

"Dang. Well, the critics will always be there. We can only do our best," Mason said.

"It's okay. I have a feeling Zipper's new article on the band will tell the truth," I responded with a slight grin. I knew that this time around, I could positively change the article's outcome.

Mason patted me on the shoulder and followed Tonya onto the stage.

"Break a leg!" I screamed.

The crowd roared when they saw Jesse's tattooed arms cusp the microphone. His raspy voice boomed into the squeaky speakers. "Thank you to everyone who came out to support us today. My name is Jesse Young, and my band is called The Matches. My drummer is Keith, Tonya's on bass, and my buddy Mason is on the keys. We also have a special guest here today," Jesse said, motioning toward Darren. "Darren helped us write our new single, 'Pitiful Peaches.' I also wanted to thank the previous band, Bret Beats, for contributing to the song. Uh…" Jesse called Mason to take over because he was at a loss of words.

Mason carefully jumped over the cords and took the microphone off the stand. The microphone screeched, and the crowd watched Jesse step back from the podium. "Hi! We are here today to celebrate James Hartley's life. Some of you may have known him, while others may not. I didn't know him. We spent time with his daughter, though. Penny, come on out."

I put one foot in front of the other. I tried not to think about how many people's eyes were locked into my side profile as I made it to the center of the stage.

Mason flashed me a genuine smile when he passed the mic into my shaking hands.

"Hello. I am Penny." My voice echoed into the throng. I was holding the microphone too close to my lips, so I pulled it away from myself. I spoke more clearly and slowly. "James was my stepdad. He was an amazing father, and he, um, loved music. Actually, I am standing here with his favorite band. My momma and I have been lost without him."

My momma wore her new Pitiful Peaches shirt in the front row. Her look of fondness gave me the courage to continue to talk. I stumbled over my words, but the audience continued listening. "Anyways. He took his life, and I try not to talk about it because people get weird when you mention suicide. But … that is why it is important to talk about it. People struggle every day, sometimes even the person who laughs and cracks the most jokes may face demons in their mind. So please check on your friends and loved ones and be kind to each other. Thanks to everyone who showed up today. I appreciate it. Enjoy the music."

The crowd clapped, and voices hollered to show their love and support. A breeze fell over my trembling body, cooling my nerves.

Familiar faces beamed up at me. I could make out the faces of Betsy, Thomas, Zach, kids from school, my co-workers, my momma, The Peach Pot crew, and Harold Hayes furiously writing in his notebook. Darren's family stood toward the very back. His father had a scowl as Doreen pulled on his belt loop, pointing at Darren behind me. She was bobbing up and down, screeching at her brother on stage. I turned around and gave Darren a thumbs-up before positioning myself out of view.

## Chapter Thirty-Three
## Hope

*Song: More Than a Feeling—Boston*
*August 1st, 1975*

The band played "Pitiful Peaches" as their opener. The crowd went wild for the song. Jesse's voice was unsteady at first, but as his confidence grew, so did his volume.

I found my mom in the crowd and danced with her. Darren's dark hair glistened when a few sweat beads fell down his face. He squinted into the distance as he prepared for his solo. He must have spotted his family. His eyes darted back to his drumsticks when Tonya, Keith, and Mason paused for Darren to hit the drums. He licked his dry lips before he began.

Darren didn't miss a beat. He hit his sticks perfectly onto the medium tom, alternating between the snare and floor tom. Jesse's hum belched over the crashing sounds. It was touching.

I peered over my shoulder to capture Gabriel nodding his head to his son's solo. Gabriel's music taste was as bland as a saltine, and he only liked gospel and some operas, but he was doing his best to support his firstborn. Darren's mother spun around, talking to people while yelling, "That's my son!"

I was proud of how far Darren, and I had come. The song ended, with all of the members taking a bow. Darren jumped off the stage to watch the rest of the concert by my side.

"Your family is here!" I yelled over the blaring music.

"I know. I can stay with you, though," he said.

"Go! Bring them up to the front."

Shortly after Darren disappeared into the horde of people, he returned with his family. Doreen squeezed my legs, pulling me into what was supposed to be a hug. She held my legs briefly while jumping up and down.

Gabriel and his wife chatted with my momma. I might have even heard him apologize for his soldier-like demeanor during the funeral preparations. Betsy and Thomas also appeared out of the crowd and alerted us that they had broken up. Betsy was already informing me about a new boy she fancied. Nothing made Betsy slow down. I thought about introducing her to my co-worker Marvin. They would probably hit it off. Thomas seemed unaffected and told me he was sorry for my loss again. Zach emerged from the crowd with the others. I was sad I barely got to see Zach the entire summer, other than at the funeral. I missed talking to him and seeing how he was.

He leaned into me to yell, "I wanted to tell you what I meant at the funeral. James and I are heavier-set guys, and I had a crush on this girl last summer. I was too embarrassed to talk to the guys about it, so I told James. He grew up chubbier and gave me some heartfelt advice that happened to work out for me. He was a good guy. I wish I could have talked to him before … you know."

"Thanks, Zach. I guess there was more to him than even I knew. If you need any advice again, I won't judge," I said, unable to give him the closure he needed.

Jesse Young and The Matches played all of James and my favorite songs. I even convinced them to play "Dive In." Most people at the event did not know their previous work. Nonetheless, many still hung around to see how much money was raised at the end of the night.

Keith put together the setlist, and he did a fantastic job. Each song flowed into the next one, forming a story of loss, love, and redemption. I hoped that he didn't have to put up too much of a fight with Jesse for it. I convinced Darren to let Doreen sit on his shoulders so she could see the stage in full motion. I loved seeing her pigtails bouncing as she took in the music. I screamed the song's lyrics as loud as I could, so James could hear me from wherever he was.

The sun started falling from the sky, and many guests began getting into their cars to leave. Mason noticed it, so the band wrapped up the last song of the evening. Jesse placed the microphone back onto the stand and went backstage to relax. Mason stood tall as he read from a notecard, "Thanks for coming out and raising money for the Hartley family. It says here that we raised a total of three thousand five hundred and twenty-two dollars!"

Momma grabbed my hands, jumping up and down in amazement. I joined her by hopping on my heels like a bunny. We would have more than enough money to pay rent, get groceries, and for momma to go to beauty school. We didn't have to return to eating buttered noodles for dinner or cut back on anything. Jesse and the band had outdone themselves. They'd changed our lives in one single night.

I would have to tell Fernando and my co-workers at Grocery Outlet that I would be working fewer hours, but they already knew. People formed a line to congratulate us on our new wealth and sent their condolences for James's death. It was also time to say goodbye to my dear friends. Betsy hugged me way too long and made me promise I would call her every week to update me on her life. Thomas talked to Darren while we discussed plans for our sophomore year.

"I don't want to let go," Betsy whined.

"It's okay. I will be okay. We can schedule a

sleepover sometime soon. I would love for you to visit over Thanksgiving break. We could have a girl's weekend with Momma and go to the real movie theater to see Elvis on the big screen," I said, hoping things wouldn't change too much.

"Oh, that's okay. I'll miss you, though! If you need absolutely anything, call me," she said, as we did our handshake for the last time.

Thomas wished me the best of luck, and Zach gave me a polite side hug when they left.

Once the field cleared, Darren got me a corndog for dinner since I had yet to eat. My stomach rumbled with hunger. My appetite for food had slowly re-emerged with time. Darren's family rented a room and left so the kids could swim in the pool before it closed for the night. We sat on the edge of the stage while we ate and observed the bright ball of light in the sky sink into the dry grass. Sunsets in Butterfield were less extravagant than the ones in Moose Creek. The air was stuffier, but it was my home. Moose Creek was a getaway, and even though I wasn't sure how I would go back, I knew I would see the cotton candy sky again one day.

Darren didn't speak as we chewed because, after all the noise from the benefit, it was time to decompress.

I swung my feet off the stage. They were dirt-covered, and my anklet needed a good scrub in the sink. I wasn't dirty per se, but it was time to get back to picking out my outfits, showering daily, and caring about my appearance instead of ignoring everything around me. I laid my head on Darren's broad shoulder, closing my eyes and taking a deep breath.

Darren grasped my face by touching my chin and bringing it up to his. He kissed me for real that time. It wasn't a quick peck or a kiss on my cheek. We pressed our lips together, opening them just enough to seep into each other. We got into the rhythm of kissing. His lips were gentle and rewarding. His dark hair was slick in my fingers, and his warm hands wrapped around my waist. A tiny yellow bird landed on the top of the stage and peered down on us, while it sang a tune of hope.

**CHAYLEE McCLEESE**

## Chapter Thirty-Four
## An End of an Era

*Song: Make Your Own Kind Of Music—Cass Elliot*
*August 1st, 1975*

The band joined us on the stage by plopping their bottoms onto the smooth black floor. Tonya sat next to me, Keith sat next to Darren, and Jesse and Mason sat on opposite ends from each other.

"That was a great show. Thanks for playing all of James's favorites," I said.

"Keith put the setlist in order, so thank him," Jesse replied.

"Well, everything you did was incredible. I can't believe we will have over three thousand dollars."

"We wanted to thank you. You helped us put some things into perspective, Penny," Mason added.

I didn't do anything other than write a stupid letter, get a job at a store, and barely get by. I couldn't imagine that I actually helped the famous Jesse Young and The Matches.

"How did I help you? I think I did more harm than good," I admitted. At the beginning of the summer, I didn't know who I was. I wasn't sure what was right or wrong. I still didn't know how to approach things when they turned from black and white to gray. I didn't know what to believe in. I knew I wanted to be nicer to people. I wanted to remind everyone I loved that they were worthy because I never knew what someone was going through. I planned to call my sister and grandma when I got home; they needed me, too.

"You helped me realize I have a problem and needed to return to my roots. We used to work so well as a band, and I lost that," Jesse said as he twiddled his thumbs back and forth. Saying something out loud made it real, and I knew how grueling it could be.

"Everyone has faults," Darren said, squeezing my hand. Squeezes were Darren and I's secret language. We talked through the tiny pinches of our flesh. It was true. Everyone had their own issues and problems; sometimes, you just had to look closer to see them.

"So, what now?" Keith asked.

"Well, school starts soon for me, and my momma will get to go to beauty school, thanks to all of you," I informed them.

"I have to head back to Moose Creek, but Tammy gave me a job at the Peach Pot to save money to come see you. She wants to spend more time with Paul, and I want to spend less time babysitting. These guys gave me a large chunk of cash from contributing to the song, so I will be back soon enough." Darren grinned.

Regardless of Moose Creek not being my summer home anymore, Darren was. Wherever Darren was, I would be, and wherever I went, he went. Our hearts were intertwined like all the numerous parts of a song.

"I am retiring," Jesse announced.

"Retiring? What do you mean you are retiring?" I asked.

"I need to step away from rock n' roll for a while. I already talked to the band, and it's a good time to take a break."

"What about touring for your new single? You can't give up," I pleaded.

Jesse explained. "I'm not giving up, but something has to change. I am going to deal with my depression and addiction head-on. I can't commit to this if I am on the road partying, meeting women, and having complete access to drugs. I think I might go visit my parents instead. I haven't seen them in years, and they will let me crash on their couch for a while."

"Is that what you really want?"

"I have to do this. It's not something I can ignore. I know it affects the band members, but if I continue down this path, I will hurt them more than if I leave to work on myself," Jesse claimed.

"Yeah, I am going to get a normal job. Your mom's dinner reminded me of when I worked at a restaurant when I was about your guys' age. I love cooking. I am grateful for everything I have been given, but fame is more than I bargained for. It will be nice to finally have some peace," Mason said.

"Yeah, unlike Mason, fame is for me. I love being on the road. A band that used to open for us asked if I could drum for them during their next tour. I probably won't see you guys for a long time. I hope everything starts looking up. Darren, if you ever need any tips for drumming let me know," Keith added.

"This is it, then?" Darren asked.

"Not really. I think we will cross each other's paths again," I said, unruffled. If there was anything that James taught me, it was that love ran deeper than blood. We were a family now.

"Not to worry, I am going to be staying around. Jesse has volunteered to help me learn how to write lyrics. I think it's time to start my own career," Tonya said.

It was sad to hear that my favorite band was splitting apart. I grew up listening to their songs with James, and a hole formed in my heart when I thought I wouldn't hear a new tune from them again. But it wasn't about what I wanted. Sometimes, what was best was not what you wanted; it was what you needed. Jesse needed this just like I required Darren, my friends, my dog Fawn, my momma, music, and the memories of James to survive. Things would always change, but I could deal with it.

Harold Hayes peeked around the corner of the stage, revealing he had been listening to our conversation the entire time. "Would all of you go on the record about what happened this summer?"

I looked at the band, and my smile spread across the stage like fire.

****

ZIPPER

*Jesse Young and The Matches Comeback and Retirement?*

By: Harold Hayes Ft. Penny Hartley

*Jesse Young and The Matches held a spectacular benefit concert in honor of James Hartley. The concert was sponsored by The Peach Pot, a rustic store located in Moose Creek, and Butterfield's local Grocery Outlet. The concert raised over a whopping $3,000 for Hartley's surviving family members, and Bret Beats and Darren Lawerence performed with Jesse Young and The Matches.*

*Bret Beats, a band that had previously intended to sue Jesse for using their sheet music, showed solidarity with the band by opening their concert in Butterfield. The band played covers of hit songs and signed over their rights of the hit single, "Pitiful Peaches" to the band and Ultimate Records.*

*Shortly after Bret's performance, Jesse Young and The Matches took the crowd by storm. Penny Hartley gave an inspiring speech about her stepdad, James, who recently passed away, and shocked the crowd with her emotional rawness, reminding everyone to be kind and check in with their loved ones. The band performed their single for the first time live, increasing their fandom.*

*An inclusive interview with Jesse revealed that he*

*did go to West-Brooke Rehabilitation Center, where he learned how to manage his anger and avoid substance abuse. He "apologizes for any harm he has caused" and plans to refund tickets for anyone who attended his show in Portland. He also revealed that he is taking a break from making music. "I need time to get back to my roots and figure my life out outside of touring. I hope I can go back on the road one day, but for now, our old albums and songs are still available to purchase. I thank my fans for their support as I face this journey," Jesse addressed the public.*

*Despite our previous beliefs, Jesse Young and The Matches have proven to be good musicians who make mistakes like the rest of us. If you want to learn more about the band and Penny's experience with them, head over to page four to read her extensive debut detailing the summer she met her favorite band, experienced her first loss, and fell in love.*

**The End**

**Evernight Teen**

**www.evernightteen.com**

www.ingramcontent.com/pod-product-compliance
Lightning Source LLC
LaVergne TN
LVHW090934080826
845145LV00003B/749

* 9 7 8 0 3 6 9 5 1 3 6 9 4 *